PROLOGUE

It was Sunday evening, and the day of rest for The Garden of Eden, the most respected and highest-priced brothel in Cudahey County, Texas, was coming to a close. The cook was on her day off, and the proprietress, Madam Ophelia, was cleaning up in the kitchen after some of the girls had taken a light supper. The madam was about to finish her chores, when she heard a gunshot somewhere outside, followed by two more in quick succession. Since gunfire was a common occurrence in Silver City, the red-light district just outside Rio Diablo, she ignored it, hoping that nothing serious had happened and that the shots were the work of a drunkenly rambunctious cowboy. She was about to blow out the lantern and go upstairs to her room, when there was a heavy thud against the back door. Startled, she froze and listened.

She heard a weak voice saying, 'Help me!'

Ophelia hesitated. Then the voice came again, its pleading tone too desperate for her to ignore. When she threw the bolt on the back door it burst open, propelled by the weight of a man leaning against it. He fell into the room, and a pistol he had been holding rattled across the floor. Through the open door, Ophelia glimpsed a shadow against the trees and bushes at the back. Shoving the man's feet out of the way, she slammed the door shut and bolted it.

5

The man appeared to be around fifty years old, and was dressed like a businessman in a dark suit and white shirt. A deep red stain was spreading rapidly over the front of the white shirt as he lay there, gasping and coughing. Ophelia bent over him and opened the front of his shirt. A wound in the left side of his chest bubbled blood when he gasped for air. He looked at her in wide-eyed desperation and tried to talk. Ophelia leaned close and with blood bubbling into his throat the man rasped, 'Clipping ... wallet ... clipping ... wallet. ...'

At first, Ophelia didn't understand but with a great effort he brought his hand up to his chest and repeated, 'Wallet.'

Ophelia reached into his inside coat pocket and drew out a large wallet. She opened it and found a yellowed newspaper clipping folded in with the money.

She asked, 'Is this it?'

The man nodded and looked relieved. He said, in a gurgling whisper, 'Finally found him ... today ... found him.' His voice trailed off and his eyes lost their focus.

Just then, two of Ophelia's girls walked into the kitchen on their way to get a snack, saw the blood and screamed.

Ophelia quietly ordered them, 'Find Shadrach, right now!'

As the girls scurried away, Ophelia thrust the newspaper clipping into her dressing-gown pocket and tried to make the man more comfortable. She found an old tablecloth and rolled it up, making a pillow that she slid under the wounded man's head. In moments, Shadrach, the light-skinned black man who served as Ophelia's bartender, bodyguard and major domo, rushed in.

'Go get the doctor and the sheriff,' Ophelia said.

Shadrach glanced at the man on the floor, nodded and walked past Ophelia. He unbolted the back door and went out, closing it behind him. Shortly, Ophelia heard the clop

6

of Shadrach's horse as he galloped away to summon help. She got hold of a clean towel and folded it into a makeshift bandage, which she placed over the bubbling chest wound. One of the girls timidly ventured back into the kitchen and asked in a tremulous voice, 'What happened?'

'Somebody shot him outside. He came to the door, looking for help,' Ophelia explained. 'Come here, press this bandage down on the wound while I loosen his collar.'

The girl did as she was told, nervously averting her eyes from the blood while Ophelia tried to lessen the unfortunate man's discomfort. She felt for the pulse in his wrist, and found it with difficulty. It was barely detectable, and as she held his wrist, the pulse stopped altogether.

Just then, she heard the front door open, the sound of heavy footsteps and to her surprise, the voice of C.J. Chalmers, Sheriff of Cudahey County. She realized that Shadrach hadn't had time even to reach town yet, but the sheriff had already arrived. She looked down and noticed that the man's wallet was open on the floor. She hastily picked it up and returned it to his inside coat pocket. She didn't want it to appear as if she had been rifling through the man's pockets.

Chalmers, a short, beer-bellied, insignificant-looking man with rheumy eyes, burst into the kitchen accompanied by one of his weasel-faced deputies.

'What's going on here?' he demanded of no one in particular.

Ophelia stood up and looked at Chalmers with ill-disguised distaste. 'Someone shot him out back. He came to the outside door and asked for help. I think he's dead.'

Chalmers snorted, and knelt by the victim. Without bothering to confirm Ophelia's opinion, he reached into the man's coat and found the wallet. He quickly opened it and sorted through it.

Looking up at Ophelia, he asked in his whiskey-raspy voice, 'Did you take anything out of here?'

Ophelia suddenly remembered the clipping, and she involuntarily started to reach for her dressing-gown pocket, but caught herself in time and put her hands on her hips. Her lips curling with disgust, she replied, '*I* don't rob corpses.'

Chalmers shot her a look of irritation, but went back to going through the man's clothes. Watching him, Ophelia became aware that the reason Chalmers was here on a Sunday night was because of the clipping she had in her pocket. He finally stood and examined the wallet again.

'His name's Martin Duke. Do you know him?'

'Never saw him in my life till he fell through that door,' Ophelia said, tilting her head toward the back door.

Squinting at Ophelia with suspicion, Chalmers asked, 'Why'd he come here?'

'How in hell should I know?' Ophelia shot back. 'We didn't have a lot of time to chew the fat, seeing as how he was shot through the lung.'

'Wha'd he say?' Chalmers pressed.

Ophelia made an effort to keep her voice steady. 'The man was dying. He tried to say something, but his lungs were filling with blood and I couldn't understand anything he said. The only thing I understood was, "Help me!" '

Chalmers looked at his deputy, and shrugged. 'Reckon there ain't nothin' else for us to do here.' He turned to Ophelia. 'Your boy was on his way to get the doctor. I 'spose the doc will haul the body up to old Grimsby's place.'

'Aren't you going out to look for whoever shot this man?' Ophelia said.

Chalmers looked surprised, then smiled. 'I figure whoever it was is long gone by now. Planned on robbin'

8

this Duke fellow, but he made it to your door 'fore that could happen.'

With that, Chalmers picked up Duke's pistol from where it had fallen and he and his deputy walked back through the parlor-room and out the front door.

After the doctor came and pronounced Mr Duke dead, Shadrach helped him load the body into the back of the buck-board. Leaving her bartender to mop up the blood on the floor of the kitchen, Ophelia wearily climbed the stairs to her room on the second floor.

Lighting her dressing-table lamp, Ophelia took the yellowed clipping from her pocket and unfolded it. The date at the top was 28 September 1880, five years ago. The column heading read 'SUSPECTED EMBEZZLER DISAPPEARS'. Two subheadings read 'Escapes with $100,000 of investors' funds' and 'Companion's whereabouts also unknown'.

The news article told about a Chicago promoter named Richard Morley, who sold shares in a California gold mine then disappeared with the investors' money. The article said that one of the investors had visited California and decided to look in on his investment and discovered that it didn't exist. His telegram back to Chicago alerted the other investors and the police. By the time the police went after Morley, he had disappeared. The story also stated that Morley was being sought for questioning about the disappearance of a young lady named Elizabeth Duke, age twenty-five, who had been his companion.

Ophelia surmised that the missing girl had been the daughter of the man who died in her kitchen. He had been seeking this Morley person for five years, and had found him in Rio Diablo. Obviously his quarry had seen him as well and made sure he would not reveal what he knew. She looked at the artist's sketch that accompanied the news story. The man depicted had a full, heavy beard that concealed a good part of his face. She stared at the

9

picture. She didn't recognize the man, but there was something about the eyes that she found vaguely familiar.

Her mind raced. What was Chalmers doing at Silver City on a Sunday night? To have arrived at the Garden when he did, he would have had to be no less than a quarter mile away when he met Shadrach. The corrupt sheriff's normal routine called for him to be at home and pleasantly drunk on Sunday night, letting his deputies handle any problems that arose.

As she sat there, a feeling of unease crept over her. 'There is something seriously wrong here,' she said to her reflection in her vanity mirror. She knew that this episode had not ended when the doc took Duke's body to the undertaker.

Ophelia rose from the dressing-table and went to the window. She looked out over the front lawn and Silver City's single street. Two cowboys, who had been drinking and gambling in one of Silver City's deadfalls, were laughing as they rode past the Garden of Eden and back toward Rio Diablo. All else was quiet.

She went to the safe in the corner of her room, opened it, and put the clipping inside. As she closed the safe door, she knew that she was in danger herself, and she shuddered when she remembered the wound in Duke's chest. But she could not know the horrendous chain of events that she had set in motion by concealing a piece of yellowed newspaper copy.

CHAPTER 1

Brimmer Stone was concentrating on writing an arrest report when Shirley Livingston, the sheriff's secretary, swayed into the room. She stood in front of his writing-table, waiting for him to look up or acknowledge her presence. When it was obvious that he was ignoring her, she put her hands on the table and leaned over, giving him a view of her *décolletage*.

'Deputy Stone,' she murmured, 'Are you ignoring me?'

'No, I'm not,' he answered, with an edge to his voice. 'I want to get this report finished before someone interrupts me.'

'My goodness,' she said plaintively, 'you were working so hard you didn't even know I was in the room.'

'Not true,' he corrected, matter-of-factly, 'I just didn't look up. I smelled your perfume.'

'Well,' she said, smiling, 'I'm glad someone likes it. I was afraid it was going to waste.'

'I didn't say I *liked* it,' Stone said brusquely. 'What's on your mind?'

She answered curtly, 'The sheriff wants to see you about a special case.'

As she huffed out of the room, pouting, Stone watched her shapely hips and could hear his father warning him, 'You don't get your meat and bread at the same store!'

11

Stone had always remembered that little maxim, and he found himself wishing that Miss Livingston's mother had told her the same thing.

When Stone walked into Dexter's office, the sheriff was waiting for him and motioned to a chair in front of his desk.

'I've got a special one for you, Stone,' he said.

'In what way special, Boss?'

'It's Randall Miller, John Jacob Miller's boy. He's got himself into a pickle,' the sheriff answered, with a frown.

'Is that any different from what he's always done?'

'Not really,' Dexter answered with a chuckle. 'This time he got caught holding out in a poker game in a downtown hotel, and instead of fessin' up and leaving the game with some dignity, he pistol-whipped the fellow that caught him. Turns out the fellow that he whipped up on is a big mucky-muck from Galveston, and after he got patched up, he decided to press charges.'

Stone grimaced unhappily. 'And you want me to pick up the boy and make sure he doesn't get hurt in the process?'

'You got it right. You're better at bringing 'em in without any holes in 'em than anyone I've got.'

'You know I don't care for this political stuff,' Stone growled. 'The old man will just pay off whoever has their hand out, and the boy will get off with a slap on the wrist.'

'I know,' Dexter answered. 'But we have to watch our backsides. That's why I want you to do it.'

With a sigh of resignation, Stone asked, 'Where is the boy now?'

'The last we heard, he was holed up down at that clutch of rat-traps on the San Jacinto River, down by the county line, Boud's Camp. You know the place?'

'Yep.' Stone was tight-lipped. 'I'm going to need eyes in the back of my head down there.'

12

'Why don't you take Skaggs with you?'

Stone fixed the sheriff with narrow eyes. 'You know how I feel about Skaggs, Sheriff; tits on a boar-hog.'

The sheriff shrugged and said, 'One more thing. It's not just whiskey that's getting the boy riled up. Somebody said he'd been taking cocaine, so be be extra careful.'

Stone had worked as a deputy sheriff in Harris County for five years, landing the job the day he turned twenty-one. He already had compiled an outstanding record of arrests that carried a high conviction rate. Moreover, he had the reputation of bringing in suspects alive, using deadly force only when it was unavoidable. He stood a sinewy six feet two in his socks, and the breadth of his shoulders and thickness of his arms hinted at the strength he had at his disposal for subduing the drunken stevedore, the hold-up man, the outraged or the deranged that seemed plentiful in the port city of Houston. Though he wore a Colt double action .45, he more frequently used the billy he carried in his hip pocket, a long pouch of thick leather loaded with double-ought buckshot and equipped with a flexible leather handle. The billy, called a slungshot in some quarters, allowed him to subdue even the most wildly belligerent suspects without shedding blood or breaking bones. These advantages, acquired along with native intelligence from his lawman father, had served him well.

Stone had the reputation of being imperturbable because of his icy calm in the face of danger and seemingly overwhelming odds. But one thing angered him and that was the nickname 'Brimstone'. His mother, who had come to Texas from the British Isles, had unintentionally burdened him with that sobriquet. Her maiden name was Moore, and she wanted to include her family name in her son's. She hit upon the old Anglo-Saxon name of Beorhtmaer, which translates to 'bright moor' and is

13

pronounced 'Brimmer' in modern English. Of course, he went by the shorter name of Brim, and when he started school it was only a matter of hours before he was being called 'Brimstone', which then changed to 'Sulfur', and, because of the proximity to the Sulpher River and the fertile Sulpher River bottoms in east Texas, the name then progressed to 'Sulfur Bottom'. It was only when Stone grew to be as big as his tormentors, and a few of them had felt his rock-hard knuckles on their noses, that the name changed back to 'Brim' or 'my friend Brim'.

It was a long ride from the midst of Houston to the river, and the heat was oppressive. As a lone rider, Stone attracted little attention until he drew near to his destination. The glances from passers-by took on a sullen aspect when he was recognized as a lawman.

By the time Stone dismounted in front of The Boud Tavern, where it was alleged Miller had been seen, the sun was low in the sky and the damp smell of Galveston Bay was heavy in the air. The buildings that made up Boud's Camp gave the impression of extensive decay. Paint that had once adorned the tavern's façade had mildewed, cracked and fallen away, as if the old boards had been stricken with a leprosy that had an affinity for yellow pine.

Stone tied his mount to the rail alongside two others. He noticed that one of them was a handsome bay, with a finely stitched saddle, out of place in such a notorious backwater. When he walked into the tavern, a miasma of tobacco, sweat and stale beer assailed his nostrils. The establishment's patrons – stevedores, dock-wallopers and various nondescripts – squinted at him as he closed the door, their curious looks quickly turning to hostile glares when they saw the badge.

Stone paused and surveyed the room. The young, moneyed gentleman he sought was not in evidence. He walked to the bar, where the bartender was busily feigning

14

nonchalance, and spoke one word: 'Miller?'

The answer was a shrug of the shoulders and a blank look.

A man sitting alone at a table in the far corner spoke up. 'Whaddya want with ma friend Miller, lawman?'

The voice was gravelly and hostile. When Stone turned, a burly man stood up. His arms and shoulders were big, but his belly was larger.

'If he's your friend, you might tell him to come along with me quietly, so he can face some charges filed on him back in Houston,' Stone said evenly.

The man's lips drew back in a bizarre smile. Two of his front teeth were missing, and those that remained were stained a yellowish brown.

'We don't give a shit what they do in Houston,' he growled.

Stone turned back to the bartender, leaning over the bar. 'As I was asking, where's Miller?'

The bartender avoided making eye contact. His eyes shifted from one side to another, occasionally to Stone's hat. 'I ain't seen 'im for a day or so. . . .'

Suddenly the barkeep's eyes focused over Stone's shoulder, and widened. Stone ducked just as a chair came crashing down, shattering on the bar where he had been standing.

From his crouched position, Stone pivoted and buried a fist in his assailant's ample belly. The man let out a muffled cry and staggered backward. Before the man could recover, Stone rose to his full height, delivering a second blow from near the floor into the bulging belly. This time his opponent doubled over. Stone brought his knee up swiftly into the man's face, breaking his nose and straightening him up, then he swung his right fist at the man's jaw, but despite the pain of a broken nose, he had seen the blow coming and blocked it with his left arm, countering it with a roundhouse right. Stone partially deflected the blow with his left upper arm, and threw a straight right into the man's chest, just over his heart. The blow staggered and confused the brute, and Stone took advantage of his hesitation by throwing another straight right to the same place. The big man, with a look of surprise, staggered into a table behind him, occupied by two drinkers. The table collapsed, and the drinkers leaped from their chairs, barely rescuing their drinks.

When his opponent stumbled backward, Stone snatched his billy from his right rear pocket. Without hesitating, he brought it down on the man's head. The first blow slowed the villain, and the second one put him on the floor, where he lay still.

Stone dragged the unconscious man to the bar, and manacled him to the brass rail. Then he turned, drew his .45 and said, 'Anyone else want to interfere with an officer of the law?'

When he received no reply, he turned and seized the bartender by his frayed and stained shirt collar, pulling him half-way across the bar. With his nose close enough to the man's face to smell his rancid breath, Stone growled, 'I know he's here. Where is he?'

Quickly deciding in favor of his own skin, the bartender cut his eyes to the left, toward the back door.

'He saw you ride up,' he whispered.

Stone released the man, who quickly stepped back against the counter behind the bar, out of the lawman's reach.

Stone opened the back door less than a half-inch, and surveyed the area behind the saloon through the crack. There was a privy, a watering-trough, a hitching rail and two outbuildings, both with open doors and dark interiors. He eased the door shut, turned and walked out the front door. He found an alley that took him behind the row of buildings, and picked his way carefully back toward the rear of the saloon. If Miller was hiding in one of those sheds, Stone hoped that surprise would allow him to take the boy into custody without using force.

He approached the nearest shed silently. There were no windows on his side of the shed and, if the Miller boy was inside, he was probably watching the saloon's back door. Stone reached the shed and carefully peered around the corner.

Suddenly, the saloon's back door burst open and one of the men who had been idling in the bar-room came out. He called, 'Randy, he's gone around to. . . .'

At that moment, the man saw Stone standing against the shed's wall, and his eyes widened. He scrambled back inside and slammed the door. Stone fell to the ground as three shots ripped through the shed wall above him, showering him with splinters. Scrambling on all fours, he gained the back of the shed and lay still.

He called out, 'Miller, give it up! No one is dead yet. Let's talk.'

Miller answered by firing another shot through the shed wall.

'Damn it, kid!' Stone shouted. 'Don't make things any worse! Put your weapon down, and come on out. We'll ride back to Houston and get this all cleared up.'

There was no reply.

The boards in the wall above him were weatherbeaten and warped. Cautiously, he raised himself to a squat so he could peer inside the shed through a crack, hoping the fading twilight would not reveal his shadow to the gunman inside. He could see a figure inside the shed, silhouetted against the open doorway. Miller, with a long-barreled pistol in his hand, was turning slowly, peering at the walls, trying to see a shadow through the cracks. When the figure turned in his direction, Stone heard a sharp intake

17

of breath and dove for the corner of the building. Two more shots rang out in rapid succession, and the shed wall was holed once again, this time where Stone had been crouching.

'That's his six,' Stone muttered, and jumping to his feet, he ran around the front corner of the shed toward the open door. Two long strides took him there, but just as he started to enter, he saw a long-barreled pistol lying in the dirt just inside the door. Instinctively, he knew that the boy would not abandon his weapon unless he had another. It was too late to stop his momentum, so he leaped across the doorway. From the corner of his eye he saw a flash inside the darkened shed, and a shot sizzled over his diving body. He hit the ground and rolled, drawing his own weapon and firing twice at knee-height through the shed wall in the approximate direction of the muzzle-flash. He heard a cry of pain and a string of obscenities, and he rolled again to change his position. At that moment, the boy charged out of the doorway, his pistol raised and firing at the ground where Stone had just been. Realizing his mistake, the boy raised his pistol, but before he could fire again, Stone squeezed off two shots into his chest.

The boy fell backward into the dirt, dropping his pistol. His body jerked several times and his heels beat a rapid tattoo on the bare earth. Then, with a rattling sigh, the body relaxed and lay still.

Stone stood up and walked to where the young man lay, kicking the pistol away from the hand that had dropped it. The young man's blue eyes were open, staring up at the darkening sky, seeing nothing. The whiskers on his chin were little more than blond fuzz. There was a ragged tear in his trouser leg, and blood was soaking the expensive wool where one of Stone's blind shots had nicked the young man's leg.

'Damn it, kid,' Stone said. 'You could have gotten off with a scar you could have bragged to the girls about. Now the good times are over.'

The curious ones from the saloon started easing through the back door, their eyes widening when they saw Miller's body.

Stone went to the saloon's rear door and walked inside. The bartender and a few remaining customers watched him in silence. The big man manacled to the brass rail raised his head and sneered, 'You're in a pile of shit now, Deputy.'

'Well, my friend,' Stone said, 'let's see how good you are with a shovel. What's your name?'

'Guy Broussard,' the man answered, pronouncing the first name to rhyme with 'key'. 'You gonna have call to 'member dat name, Deputy.'

'I'll try to remember it, so we can file you under the right name, Broussard.'

With that, he bent down and unlocked the manacle from the brass rail. Holding his pistol on his prisoner, he said, 'My guess is that the bay with the fancy saddle out there is the kid's horse.'

When Broussard nodded, Stone said, 'Let's go.'

Stone instructed his prisoner to take the bay and lead it around to the back of the saloon. There, he had Broussard load the boy's body on to the horse and then climb into the saddle. Stone manacled Broussard's right arm to the corpse's left arm, and they started to Houston with their sad cargo.

It was late by the time they reached the sheriff's office. No one was on duty, except a junior deputy and the gaoler. Stone turned Broussard over to the gaoler to be locked up until he could be charged the next morning with assaulting a law officer. He then took the body of young Randall Miller to the coroner's office.

Stone knew that the boy's death would have repercussions, so he returned to the office, put on a pot of coffee and started writing out his report. By the time the sun rose, he had finished the report. Rather than put off the inevitable confrontation with the sheriff, Stone stayed at his desk until Dexter reported for work.

When the sheriff walked in and saw Stone, he knew something was wrong. He tilted his head toward his office and walked away. After a few minutes, Stone followed. He went over the entire incident, including the arrest of Broussard, and turned over Miller's two pistols, a .44 rimfire Colt with an eight-inch barrel, and a new, nickel-plated Smith & Wesson double action .32.

When Stone finished his narrative, Dexter sat without speaking, head down, staring at the top of his desk. Finally, he sat up and looked around the office, as if seeing it for the first time.

'Well, I might as well ride on out and give John Jacob Miller the bad news,' he murmured. 'Damn, I hate this! You know there's goin' to be a shit-pot full of trouble don't you?'

'I know, Sheriff,' Stone answered softly. 'As you'll recall, I didn't want the job.'

'I know,' the sheriff agreed. 'If I had sent someone else, I'd probably have a dead deputy floating in the San Jacinto right now.' Shaking his head he added, 'Some days you just can't win.'

Wearily, the sheriff got up and put on his hat. 'Shirley,' he called to his secretary, 'I'm going to be out of the office for a while. I'll be out to J.J. Miller's place.'

Turning to Stone, he said, 'Why don't you go on home and get some sleep? I've got a feeling you're going to need it.'

CHAPTER 2

The prospect of returning to his room at the boarding-house struck Stone as being about as inviting as lying in a sunken grave. He thought of Marissa, and he turned and headed toward the west side of town.

He was well known in the heavily Latino neighborhood where Marissa lived, and he returned frequent greetings from smiling residents. He tied up his horse in front of Marissa's modest home and walked to the door.

He was about to rap, when Marissa appeared at the door and squealed '*Breemer!*' She flung open the door and stretched her arms around his neck, turning up her face for his kiss.

After the kiss, she looked into his eyes with concern and said, 'You are here in the middle of the morning, and you look tired, my love. *Que pasa?*'

'I have had a very long night, and I had to kill someone that I did not wish to kill,' he explained.

Marissa clasped his right hand in hers and kissed it in sympathy.

'My body is tired, but my brain is even more tired,' he continued. 'I didn't want to go to my room and be alone with my conscience, so I came here. I am shamelessly taking advantage of your affection for me, and I am asking if you would be angry if I stayed and slept in your bed?'

21

She smiled up at him, her dark eyes sparkling. 'Have I ever refused you my bed?' she teased.

After he put his horse in the shed at the back of the house, he walked into the bedroom and started undressing. He stripped down to his underwear and climbed into the bed.

Marissa lay beside him and put her left arm around him, pressing her breasts into his back. She could feel the tension in his body slowly fading.

He said softly, 'No matter what happens, you make me feel better. You are precious to me, Marissa.'

They lay there quietly for a while.

'Do you want to make love?' she asked.

There was no answer, only his steady, deep breathing. She smiled to herself and snuggled up closer, enjoying his warmth and the smell of his perspiration.

When he awoke, it was evening and Marissa was gone to her job at the tavern. He dressed, left a note for Marissa, and rode slowly back to his boarding-house.

As Stone rode up to the boarding-house, a figure rose from a rocking chair on the darkened front porch. Stone's hand went to his pistol and rested there.

There was a shout, and a familiar voice cried, 'Brimmer Stone, you old law-dog, you still sloppin' at the public trough?'

It was Grady Henderson, an old friend of his youth and companion on cattle drives from Texas to Kansas and points north. After whoops of greeting, backslaps and good-natured insults, they decided to go to a nearby saloon, where they could talk and catch up.

The two had shared long days on the trail with their dust, blizzards, wild animals and stampedes. They were the same age, but in years only. Grady had successfully avoided mental maturity, and charged headlong, like an eighteen-year-old, into almost everything, including romance. Many young ladies found his blue eyes, black curly hair and spontaneous sense of humor to be irresistible, and he took full advantage of their proclivities. His problem was that he failed to discriminate between ladies who were unattached and those with inconvenient encumbrances such as husbands. Stone had always told Grady that he should start thinking with his brain instead of his pecker, which was always leading him into trouble. He had frequently pointed out to Grady that he couldn't always be around to throw him a rope and haul him out of the holes he kept digging for himself.

They ordered beers, and Grady explained he had been on the trail for the better part of a year in various parts of the country and had just returned to Houston. He was effusive and full of stories about his latest trail drive, telling tales of his friends' drinking, whoring and losing at faro. Then he grew serious.

'Brim, I've been thinking about this trail drive business a lot lately, and I think I may want to do something else.'

'There's nothing wrong with that,' Stone answered. 'Maybe you're finally growing up.'

'You think so, Brim?' Grady beamed. 'Because I'm thinkin' about gettin' a regular job and settlin' down.'

'Now that *is* a surprise!' Stone said, amazed.

Grady looked across the room as if he was seeing something in the distance.

'Brim,' he said, choosing his words carefully, 'on my last drive, we lost one of the hands in a stampede. Dusty was a hell of a nice fellow, laughed and joked all the time, and everyone liked him. One bad night up in the territories, we had a stampede. After we finally got 'em turned in on themselves and got 'em to milling, when the sun come up we were a man short. One of the hands rode back up the trail and found Dusty. His horse must have stepped in a prairie

23

dog hole and fell. About half the herd must have run over him and his horse. Anyway, we got him picked up the best we could, and buried him alongside the trail. We stuck a wooden marker up on his grave, with his name and the date he died. We didn't know his birth date or whether or not he had any family. You know we've buried friends before, but when we rode off this time, I looked back at that grave and I got the damnedest feeling in the pit of my stomach.'

Grady looked at Brim with moist eyes. 'Brim, I don't want to be buried by the side of a trail someplace and forgotten. When I go, I want to be buried in a graveyard, with a decent headstone and my family there to mourn for me.'

'Sounds only reasonable to me,' Brim replied. 'And I reckon there's no time like the present to do something about it.'

Grady appeared relieved, and he smiled. 'So you don't think I'm a nance for wantin' to quit trail driving?'

'Hell, no,' Brim answered. 'Like I said, I think you're finally growing up.'

'What about you, Brim?' Grady asked. 'What do you want to do with your life? You going to stay a lawman?'

Stone explained the entire story about Randall Miller and his father, and that he was awaiting the outcome of the sheriff's meetings. 'Right now, I'd say my future is a little up in the air,' he added.

Grady was indignant. 'By damn, they can't do that to you, Brim! What in hell's gone wrong with the law system?'

'I'm afraid the law has very little to do with it, Grady. A Mexican friend of mine summed it up for me one time. He said, "*Dios es omnipotente, y el dinero es su tiniente.*" *

Grady leaned back in his chair, amazed. 'I tell you what, Brimmer old pal, if they stick it to you, tell 'em to go to hell, and let's you and me light out for Rio Diablo.'

---

* God is all-powerful, and money is his lieutenant.

Stone smiled at the memory of Rio Diablo, a wide-open town in north Texas, where the two of them had sown some youthful wild oats.

'It would be a change. But why Rio Diablo?'

'Well, I got my reasons,' Grady answered, an impish smile curling his lips.

Two days later, an unhappy Sheriff Baxter called Stone into his office and said, 'Stone, John Jacob Miller had no more consigned his son's body to the sod and his soul to the Lord, than he started pressing the District Attorney to file murder charges on you. He went bail for that Broussard fellow who you dragged in here, and that gaol-bird is willing to testify that you shot down Randall Miller in cold blood.'

Stone was not surprised. 'You have my report, Sheriff. It's all there. Broussard was manacled to the brass rail in the saloon. He didn't see a thing.'

'I know, so I sent Jackson and Harper out to Boud's Inlet to look at the scene. That shack that Miller was hiding in has been torn down, and the lumber burned. So there's no physical evidence to back up your story. J.J. Miller didn't get rich by overlooking the details.'

Anger flickered over Stone's face. 'So, they're setting me up for a frame. What's next?'

'I'm on my way to talk to the District Attorney. He's not too happy about this, but he's got to do something. The county commissioners are making a stink, too. But I'm not worried about that, I've got something on all of them.'

'I appreciate you sticking up for me,' Stone said.

'You're the best man I have, Stone. I'm damn well going to stick up for you. If I didn't, what kind of lawman would I be?'

Late in the day, an exhausted Sheriff Baxter returned to his office and sent for Stone. When Stone walked in, the sheriff's countenance told him that the news was not good.

'Stone,' the sheriff said, 'I've been with the District Attorney, the Mayor and the county commissioners all day. I won't go into the details, but I can guarantee there were some threats made there today. The long and short of it is the deal I finally cut with them, that you resign and leave the county, and they forget about the grand jury, and I get to keep my job.'

The sheriff paused, looking down at his desk. When he raised his head to look at Stone, his eyes were reddened and moist. 'I can't tell you how sorry I am, Stone.'

Stone sat silently, letting the sheriff's words sink in. Finally he said, 'So money talks louder than justice. Is that it, Sheriff?'

The sheriff looked at him with pain in his eyes. 'That's it, Stone.'

Stone took the badge off his vest, put it on the sheriff's desk and stood up.

'Sheriff,' he said in a low rumble, 'I suppose I've been living in a fool's paradise this last five years. I thought if a man did his job, kept his nose clean and told the truth, he'd always come out on top. I was wrong as hell, and I don't intend ever again to put myself in a position where money and politics count more than justice.'

The sheriff smiled. 'Well, Stone, I reckon you won't be working in a law job.'

'If this is what I can expect,' Stone answered, 'I reckon not.'

That night, Grady asked, 'How long will it take for you to finish up your business here and be ready to hit the trail?'

Stone answered, 'A couple of days ought to do it.'

'How about Marissa?' Grady wondered.

'Yeah, Marissa. I suppose I'd better go over and tell her

the news. That isn't going to be easy,' Stone said glumly.

'If you don't mind, pardner, I'll let you do that on your own.'

Stone found Marissa at the Taberna Felix, where she sang and danced five nights a week. To Stone's surprise, she had already heard about what had happened.

'How did you hear so fast?' he asked.

Marissa looked at him with tears starting from her eyes. 'Everyone here knows you and respects you. They hoped that you would someday be *jefe*. Many of them are angry.'

'That makes me very proud to be thought of that way,' Stone said. 'I'm sorry that we all must be disappointed.'

Marissa gazed at him with stricken eyes. 'Did you come to say goodbye?'

'No. Not yet. I just came to tell you I would be leaving on Thursday morning. I want to see you on Wednesday night. We'll say goodbye then.'

As he left the taberna, Stone noticed an Anglo loafing about outside. He had seen the man before, and knew him as a thug and minor grifter. He walked up to the man, who looked surprised and glanced about, looking for an escape route.

'My friend,' Stone said, 'don't you know you stand out too much in this part of town? You should tell Miller that if he wants me trailed down here, he needs to hire a Latino. That is, if he could find one dishonest enough to do it.'

The man looked stunned, and stammered, 'I don't know what you're talking about.'

'Don't stay too close behind me,' Stone added. 'It makes me nervous.'

Stone mounted his horse and rode away, leaving the man staring after him.

On Wednesday night at ten o'clock, Stone walked out of his boarding-house for the last time and mounted his horse for the ride to Marissa's. He knew he had been shadowed over the past three days, and this night was no exception. A lone horseman loosely trailed him as he rode through the Houston streets on the way to Marissa's place. To make it easy for his shadow, he took his customary route to the south-east part of town. Before he reached Marissa's neighborhood, he saw that his shadow no longer trailed him, and he smiled with satisfaction. Immediately changing his route, he trotted to a blacksmith's shop a block away from Marissa's home.

As he rode up, the smithy, Jesus de la Torre, greeted him with a smile.

'Hello, my friend, this is an unexpected pleasure. What brings you here?'

'I need a favor, Chuy,' Stone said. 'Can I leave my horse here for the night?'

'Sure you can. *Que pasa?*'

'Just between me and you,' Stone answered, 'I've got to sneak up on somebody.'

After seeing to his horse, Stone walked away up the street into the darkness. His path took him to a brushy spot behind Marissa's modest frame home. Immediately, he found a horse tied to a bush, peacefully grazing. Carefully, he picked his way through the brush, staying in the shadows as much as possible, until he reached a vantage place perhaps twenty-five yards behind the dwelling. There, he crouched down and peered into the darkness around the house. After a few minutes, he saw a movement in the shadows beside the house.

Stone picked his way carefully through the scattered bushes. Two horsemen suddenly galloped down the street in front of Marissa's house, crying out to one another and laughing. Stone took advantage of the noise to move up behind his quarry undetected. By the faint light from the window he could make out that it was Skaggs. Stone drew his sidearm and cocked the hammer. The metallic click had the effect of a thunderbolt on Skaggs. His body lurched and his hands went into the air.

'Don't kill me! Don't kill me!' he pleaded.

'Turn around,' Stone ordered.

Skaggs turned to face Stone. He stared at the barrel of Stone's six-shooter. Perspiration stood out on his forehead in the faint light.

'Drop your gun-belt,' Stone commanded, and the belt fell to the ground.

'Now take off that badge.'

With trembling fingers, Skaggs removed the badge from his shirt and dropped it beside the gun-belt.

'There's always one rotten apple,' Stone said. 'I always thought you were easily bought, Skaggs. Now you've proved it. Now turn around and start walking. If you make it out of this neighborhood alive, you can tell Mr Miller that you screwed up. If you try to come back here, I will kill you. Now get going!'

Relief flooded his face, and Skaggs turned and ran without looking back.

Stone picked up the badge and gun-belt. He would have Chuy send them back to the sheriff tomorrow with an explanatory note. Stone had too many things on his mind to waste time on Skaggs.

Stone rapped lightly on Marissa's door. She opened it, wearing a white cotton shift that was thin enough for him to see more than a subtle suggestion of the body beneath it. She was combing out her waist-length hair, which was black as a raven's wing.

'Breemer!' she sighed, pronouncing his name in her own way. '*Mi corazon*. I was afraid you would not come.'

Taking her in his arms, he kissed her deeply, feeling the

29

firm softness of her skin through the simple shift. He could smell the soap from the bath she had just finished and her hair was damp. Her full lips responded hungrily and she pressed her body to his. He could feel the excitement flooding through his body.

She was small, five feet four, blessed with a figure in the Mexican ideal: shapely breasts proportional to her frame and rounded, generous hips that Brim found irresistible.

When the long, deep kiss ended, he asked, 'Why did you think I would not come?'

'Because you are leaving tomorrow, and you hate my tears.'

'Hate your tears? I don't hate your tears, I *fear* them,' he said softly. 'When I cause your tears, every one of them pierces my heart like a knife.'

She smiled. 'No, you are now the Anglo *vaquero*. You travel across the country and meet a girl in every town. And you break her heart, too.'

'No, you know that's not true, not of me. Grady perhaps, but not me.'

'*Ay!*' she answered, making a wry face at the thought of Grady. '*El machisto!*'

'Anyway, I'm here as you can see. Let's don't talk about goodbyes, not yet. We have tonight. I'll go in the morning, at first light.'

She put her arms around his neck and brought her mouth up to his. The scent, warmth and softness of her excited him, and he pulled her closer.

'No, not yet,' she said. 'We have time.' She turned and walked into the modest kitchen. 'We will have something to eat, and you can have your tequila and we will talk.'

She brought in a plate of charcoaled strips of cabrito, and large crisp tacos. She put a bottle of tequila and a small glass beside the plates.

'I'm sorry my hair is still wet. I had to wash it before you

30

came. When I sing in the taberna, my hair stinks of tobacco smoke.'

They sat and ate the tasty meat, and Brim had his customary two drinks of tequila.

They talked of her father Conozco, who mistrusted Anglos and was a barrier between them, for Marissa would never think of marrying Stone while her father was alive. They spoke of her brother Sinecio, the businessman, and they discussed the taberna where she worked. She talked of Señor Guitierez, her boss, or *el patron*, as she called him. They conversed about the powerful man who was responsible for Stone leaving, and she muttered a dark curse against him and his children with tears in her eyes. When they had finished eating, Marissa cleared the table and wiped it clean.

In the bedroom, they moved with the relaxed familiarity of old lovers. Stone sat on the bed and pulled off his boots. Sitting gracefully in the middle of the bed, Marissa pulled the shift up over her head and let it drop to the floor, a gesture that Stone found almost unbearably exciting. He rolled over and took her in his arms, kissing her quivering lips time and time again, feasting on the spicy sweetness of her. There was an unaccustomed urgency to her lovemaking, almost desperation, as if she were trying to make up in advance for his absence from her arms.

They made love three times during the night and finally fell asleep, exhausted.

The next morning, as the sun lightened the horizon, Brim dressed quietly and went to the door, opening it carefully so as not to waken her. But as he went through the door, she spoke softly from the bed, her words piercing his chest like a dagger, '*Vaya con Dios, alma de mi corazon.*'*

* Go with God, soul of my heart.

31

CHAPTER 3

On the ride from Houston to Rio Diablo, Stone learned to his surprise that the 'lady' who held Grady's interest worked at one of the brothels in the notorious area of Silver City, just outside town.

'Are you serious about marrying this girl?' he asked in amazement. 'After all, she's been whoring for a while now. She's what my mama would have called "damaged goods".'

'I know, Brim. But when we're together, it's different than when I'm with another girl. How can I put it? Our minds just kind of fit together. That's a hell of a feeling. Never had it with anyone else.' Growing serious, Grady added, 'Brim, you know I've been with a lot of ladies . . '

'Yeah, I know,' Stone said, rolling his eyes. 'Seems I remember getting you out of a few tight spots because of those *ladies*, as you call 'em.'

'I liked most of 'em, too.'

'Yeah, you were always in love with the one you were with.'

Ignoring Stone's jibe, Grady continued. 'But I have never had one who I liked so much up here,' he said, tapping his forehead.

Stone frowned and shook his head in disbelief. 'It must be serious if you like her for her mind, because it would sure as hell be the first time you ever gave any thought to *that* end of a woman!'

The long ride to Rio Diablo was uneventful. The horse-men stayed in hotels when one could be found, and slept under the stars in their bedrolls when nothing else, such as a hayloft, was available. They finally arrived on the crest of a hill south of Rio Diablo. In the wooded valley below them, they could see a few buildings and the spire of a church.

Rio Diablo had been founded, or festered, depending on the observer's moral point of view, just south of the Red River at the junction of the Butterfield overland mail route and a branch of the Chisholm Trail – major routes for settlers and businessmen braving the rigors of the great south-west to travel to the promised land of California. It was a convenient jumping-off place for those traveling to the Oklahoma wilds from the major centers of commerce to the south. Though farming and ranching supplied the livelihood for the bulk of the local popula-tion, the town was a haven for trail drivers and the cowboys who worked vast herds in the Oklahoma territory, laborers on their way west, mule-skinners, cotton-buyers and gandy dancers who maintained the railroads that carried the county's products to market. The town's business district comprised seven blocks from east to west along California Street. Four blocks of that were given over to twenty-one saloons of varying worth and reputation, forming a 'no-lady's-land', where a respectable female dared not tread.

It was said by the old-timers that the town's original settlers had intended to call their enclave Rio Rojo, after the nearby Red River. But as the town grew, it became a hotbed of fugitives from the law, gamblers and prostitutes, who came to outnumber the original hard-working settlers. When it came time to obtain a state charter and a post office, the mayor, a saloon- and brothel-operator, declared the name Rio Rojo too pedestrian for his boom-ing Gomorrah, and listed the town's name as Rio Diablo.

Afterward, more and more farmers moved into the county, the flamboyant mayor's mistress emptied a six-shooter into him for unfaithfulness, and a more God-fearing, sedate cabal took over City Hall.

Stone and Grady checked in to the Cowboys' Rest Hotel on the west end of California Street, and wasted no time in getting a hot bath. While they were cleaning up, Grady reminded Stone of Barbara Carrington.

Smiling at the memory, Stone said, 'Barbara Carrington. Good-looking, but a little skinny. She was from good folks, and was scared to death that her father was going to find out she was keeping company with a drover. She's more than likely married with a batch of young'uns by now.'

To change the subject, Stone asked, 'So, you're going to go see that whore tonight?'

Grady, irritated, answered, 'Her name is Jorene. And you can bet I'm going to see her tonight.'

After dressing, Stone went down to the lobby and asked the desk-clerk if he knew of the Carrington family, the people who owned the cotton gin.

The desk-clerk knew the family, said that Mr Ebenezer Carrington died about a year ago and that the daughter had inherited. He added that she still owned the cotton gin and the warehouse, but her uncle managed them.

'What became of the daughter?' Stone enquired. 'Has she married?'

'No sir,' the desk-clerk answered. 'She's not married yet, but it's not because she ain't had the opportunity. Every single man in town has been after her. She's a good-looking woman and rich to boot. Runs a little business downtown, kind of like a hobby. It's the millinery shop across from the Imperial Hotel. Would be quite a catch,' he added, raising his eyebrows.

Obtaining some stationery from the clerk, Stone

penned a note to Barbara Carrington. It read: 'May Mr Brimmer Stone call upon Miss Barbara Carrington this evening?' Sealing the note in an envelope, he asked the desk-clerk if he had the means to deliver a message. The desk-clerk summoned a young boy called Newt from a small room behind the office.

'Do you know Miss Carrington who works at the millinery store down by the big hotel?' Brim asked the boy.

'Shoot, yes,' the lad answered happily, his blue eyes shining. 'The purty lady. Everybody knows her.'

Stone gave the boy a five-cent piece and the note. 'Wait for an answer,' he instructed. The boy scurried out the door.

While waiting for an answer, Stone and Grady had their supper in the hotel's modest dining-room. They were eating when the boy returned.

'Did the lady answer?' Stone asked.

Grinning broadly, Newt nodded his head vigorously. 'Yessuh, she did,' he replied. A note was not in evidence.

Stone grunted, and pulled out another five cents, and then the note materialized from Newt's back pocket.

As Newt departed, Stone opened the note and started reading, raising one eyebrow.

'Wha'd she say?' Grady asked.

'Listen to this,' Stone said, reading the note aloud. 'Mr Brimmer Stone, you son of a bitch! Do you think you can just have your way with me and then ride away and not even say goodbye, and then ride back into town unannounced and ask if you can come calling?'

Grady's eyes widened. 'Didn't turn out too well, did it?' he sniggered.

'There's more,' Stone said, reading the last line. 'You can apologize for your shabby treatment of me if you come to my mother's house at nine o'clock tonight.'

Stone folded up the note and put it in his shirt pocket,

a smug look on his face. 'I reckon I'd better invest in a bunch of flowers before I show up.'

Grady shook his head, grinning. 'You are one lucky cowboy,' he chuckled. He thought for a moment, then said, 'Or the best damn note-writer in Texas!'

Stone sought out a source for a bouquet of flowers, and dropped by the mercantile for a box of candy. Leaving his peace offerings in the hotel room, he agreed to accompany Grady to Silver City for a call on Jorene.

'Does she know you're coming?' he enquired.

Grady nodded. 'On my last drive, we stopped at Doan's Store just before crossing the Red River. I sent her a letter from there telling her I might be dropping by in September or October. So I reckon she's at least half-way expectin' me.'

They walked next door to the stable, saddled up their horses and rode out to Silver City. They tied their horses in front of The Garden of Eden, the highest-toned of the Silver City fancy-houses.

They walked into the gaily decorated parlor to be greeted by Madam Ophelia. The lady was resplendent in a gown of emerald green, a head-dress of feathers in matching and complementary hues, and elbow-length pearl-colored gloves. She swept down on the two travelers, greeting them as if they were the sons of John Jacob Astor.

'Good evening, gentlemen,' she gushed. 'It's indeed a pleasure to have two such manly and handsome visitors to our humble home.'

Stone glanced around the 'humble home'. The walls were covered with red wallpaper, accented by a design of golden hearts pierced by tiny arrows. The overstuffed chairs were of red or purple velvet, and gilt sconces held the kerosene lamps.

Several of the house's inmates were seated at the far end of the parlor, chatting quietly. Just as Madam Ophelia was asking her visitors what their pleasures might be, there was a squeal from the end of the room, and a voice cried, 'Grady!'

Within a moment, a blonde young lady had leaped into Grady's arms and started smothering him with kisses. Taken aback, Madam Ophelia allowed the gentle assault to continue for a few moments, then cleared her throat for attention.

Hastily composing herself, Jorene said, 'Grady, this is Madam Ophelia, the lady that runs this place. Ma'am, this here is Grady Henderson, the fellow I told you about.'

'Howdy, ma'am,' Grady said. 'This big fellow here is Brimmer Stone.'

Madam Ophelia nodded, smilingly appraising Stone while Jorene said, 'My goodness, you're a pretty one. The girls are just goin' to *love* you.'

Smiling under the scrutiny, Stone said, 'Truth is, ma'am, that I won't be, er, I won't be staying. . . .'

Grady laughed. 'What he's trying to say is that he's got a rendezvous with a lady in Rio Diablo tonight.'

'In other words,' Jorene observed, 'he's gettin' it for free.'

'That remains to be seen,' Stone answered, to raucous laughter.

As Grady paid Madam Ophelia for Jorene's time, and the two of them went upstairs, Stone bid a polite goodbye to The Garden of Eden and rode back toward town.

The October night had turned cool when Brim retrieved his peace offerings at the hotel and rode east down California Street, past the numerous saloons, all of which seemed to be in full swing. From one, there was the sound of a tinny piano; from another, the rattle of the roulette ball and the shouts of the gamblers.

Brim turned off California Street and rode south on Lindsay Avenue into a residential area. He remembered precisely where the house was. He had never been allowed inside, but he knew the place that Barbara referred to as 'my mother's house', though her mother had been dead several years. It was a dignified, well-maintained, two-story gingerbread.

Brim yanked on the bell-pull and heard the ringing inside the house. In a few moments, Barbara herself opened the door. She was no longer the skinny, gangling but pretty girl that Brim remembered. The face had matured to that of a striking woman. She had full lips, and her luxuriant, chestnut-colored hair hung past her shoulders. She was a statuesque five feet eight or nine, with a full bosom. The dress she wore was tasteful, revealing only a hint of breast and accentuating her slender waist. Her snapping, dark brown eyes warned the admirer, while still holding out promise.

'You brought flowers, how nice,' she said, taking the flowers and candy and placing them on the hallway table. Then she turned around and delivered a roundhouse slap to Stone's left cheek.

'Damn, woman, what was that for?' he exclaimed, rubbing his cheek.

'That's for being my first lover and then riding away out of my life and not even saying goodbye!'

'I told you I couldn't handle goodbyes. That's why I left like I did.'

'I was an eighteen-year-old girl. I was in love with you.' The hurt in her voice was obvious.

'I wasn't much more than a boy myself. I didn't understand much about love and how the world works.' Stone managed to sound contrite. 'I'm sorry for hurting you. If it means anything, it hurt me to leave, too.'

'How long will you be in Rio Diablo?' she asked, brushing his apology aside.

'I don't know,' he answered, frowning. 'I'm no longer a

lawman in Harris County. Been riding with Grady, trying to figure out what to do next. May be around here a while.'

'Then I suppose you can kiss me hello,' she said, pressing close and raising her mouth to his.

She didn't hold back, and feeling her in his arms pressed close to his body was worth the discomfort of the long trip through Texas. The sensation of her mouth on his told him that the tentative, hesitant girl he had known was, in every sense, now a mature woman. The sudden change in her mood confused Stone.

When the kiss ended, she said, 'Let's sit in front of the fire, have a drink and talk for a while.'

She led him into the parlor, where a small fire was burning in the fireplace against the evening chill.

Stone glanced around. 'Are you living here by yourself?'

'No,' she answered, smiling, 'but I sent the help away for the evening.'

They sat on the large couch before the fire, sipped an excellent wine and talked. Stone told her of his career as a lawman, and the circumstances that brought it to an end. He told her that on the ride to Rio Diablo, he had taken the time to size things up and he had decided he might consider getting back into law work in the right place.

Barbara laughed, a deep down in the throat laugh, low and husky. 'If you want law work, we've got enough in this town for ten lawmen! Ten *honest* lawmen, that is.'

'You telling me that the sheriff is not on the up and up?'

'That's what I'm telling you, but I don't want to talk about that now, maybe later,' she whispered.

She put down her wineglass and leaned toward him. She put both arms around his neck and put her lips on his. The kisses were long, deep and wet. She kissed him almost hungrily. He kissed her ears and her throat, kissing down to where her breasts swelled above the tight bodice of the dress she wore. She was breathing heavily when she suddenly stood. Her face was flushed as she looked down at Stone's expression of disappointment and bewilderment.

'No,' she said. 'I'm not giving in to you after you've been out of my life for six years and you've been back an hour. I knew an eighteen-year-old boy. I don't know the man.'

Stone stood. 'I understand,' he said softly. 'I suppose we had better get to know one another before, well, before. . . .'

'Being intimate?' she said, finishing the thought for him.

'Yes, of course,' he said. 'We're supposed to be more responsible now, aren't we?'

He got his hat and turned to go.

'Tomorrow?' he asked.

'Tomorrow,' she answered, kissing his cheek.

Stone took his leave and rode slowly back to California Street as he pondered his visit with Barbara Carrington. He had assumed that she would be married by this time, and had been pleasantly surprised that she was not. He felt a twinge of conscience when he thought of his last night with Marissa as Barbara's taste and scent lingered on his lips.

When he reached the main street, Stone slowed his mount to a gentle trot and turned west. Rio Diablo's business district was quiet, but the stretch of saloons just beyond was wide awake. Range hands, mule-skinners and scores of worthies of various stripes milled in and out of the saloons. The notes of a banjo or piano seeped past the swinging doors of some establishments, accompanied by raucous laughter or loud cursing. Names of the saloons ran the gamut from the picturesque to the bizarre, such as The Bluebonnet, Iron Mike's and The Pig's Elbow.

As Stone neared the center of the saloon district, he noticed some activity at a large saloon called The Lone Star. A well-groomed man in his thirties was escorting a loudly protesting cowboy through the front door to the boardwalk. Upon reaching the boardwalk's edge, the bouncer abruptly shoved the cowboy into the street. As Stone reined to a stop, the cowboy fell into the dirt and immediately jumped to his feet, cursing. He faced the man who had shoved him, and reached for his pistol. Before he could get the weapon clear of the holster, the bouncer had drawn his own pistol and had it pointed at the cowboy's chest. The cowboy, astounded by the speed with which his opponent had drawn, froze, his pistol half-way out of the holster. The bouncer's face curled into a smile, and the cowboy jammed his weapon back into the holster in surrender. For a moment, Stone thought the episode was over and that the cowboy, made to look fool-ish, would turn and walk away. But before he could take a step, the bouncer fired. The cowboy pitched backward into the street, twitched a few times, then lay still.

Stone was aghast at the cold-blooded murder he had witnessed. He sat watching as a scruffy-looking character wearing a badge walked off the boardwalk and leaned over the fresh corpse.

The bouncer said, 'He drew on me, deputy.'

The deputy looked up from his inspection of the deceased and said, 'You're absolutely right, Mr Smith. I seen the whole thing.'

The gunman called Smith turned to walk back into the saloon. A man who appeared to be the same age as the gunman, and dressed in the same quality clothes, smiled and turned to accompany him. A crowd of the curious started gathering around the body, and Stone spurred his mount and hurried away from the scene.

CHAPTER 4

The next morning, Stone and Grady decided to go for breakfast at 'Mom's', which was sandwiched between two saloons, about half-way through the saloon district. Leaving their guns in the hotel safe, they strolled leisurely up California Street, taking in the sights, sounds and odors.

They walked past several evil-smelling saloons on the way, but found that Mom's place smelled like coffee and frying bacon. No sooner had they found a table against the wall in the long and narrow eatery, when a sizable, gray-haired lady wearing gingham and an apron put two mugs of coffee on the table.

'What's your pleasure, buckaroos?' she said, in a whiskey-raspy voice.

'What's the specialty of the house?' Grady asked.

'Three fried eggs, a ham steak, grits, red-eye gravy and biscuits for thirty cents,' she answered.

Grady looked at Stone and said, 'We'll each have that.'

Mom shuffled back to her grill, while Stone and Grady sipped their coffee.

Grady looked at his cup and made a face. 'Seems kinda weak after that Arbuckle you get on a drive,' he observed.

Stone laughed at the memory. 'Grady, after that boiled trail-drive coffee, lye soap would taste weak.'

They started talking and laughing about the bad-tempered trail cooks they had known, when a large, blond man wearing a deputy's badge walked in. His lower lip drooped, and his eyes wore a vacant expression. Stone noticed he was wearing an old Army Colt .44 converted to fire metallic cartridges. The deputy walked to their table and fixed Stone with a stare.

'Haven't seen you two round here before. What are you doing in Rio Diablo?' he growled.

Stone glanced back at Mom, who was standing at her grill regarding the deputy with contempt. He looked at the deputy and answered in a pleasant tone, 'Right now, having breakfast.'

'Where'd you come here from?' the deputy asked, in a suspicious tone.

Stone regarded the man for a few moments, then said sarcastically, 'Well, you might say we came from Houston, but my friend here spent some time in Dodge City and an awful lot of time in the Oklahoma territories. So take your pick.'

The deputy's eyes narrowed as he tried to take in Stone's words. 'You're some kind of a smart-ass . . .'

'Look, deputy, that badge gives you some authority, but it doesn't include giving honest people a load of shit. Now unless you're going to charge us with a crime or suspicion of one, we'd appreciate it if you'd leave us alone so we can eat our biscuits.'

The deputy's face reddened, and he went for his sidearm.

Without rising from his chair, Stone reached over with his left hand and clamped the deputy's wrist before he could pull the weapon. With his right, he slugged the big man in the crotch.

With a groan, the deputy grabbed his vitals with both hands and folded up on the floor. Stone got up, removed

43

the deputy's .44 from its holster and put it on the table, then dragged the big man to the door by his shirt collar. Leaving him on the boardwalk, Stone said, 'If you want that old thumb-buster back, send the sheriff for it.'

He walked back into Mom's and sat down at his table. Grady had not budged from his chair, and Mom was laughing raucously.

'By damn,' she said, 'I'm glad I got to see that! That big dumb bastard has been bullying people in this town for three years. His name is Luther Boggs, and he's the sheriff's nephew. It's the only job he's ever held for more than a week.'

They were finishing their breakfasts when the door opened and a pot-bellied man in a large white hat and wearing a sheriff's badge walked in. He picked up a chair, spun it around, and sat down at their table, resting his arms on the chair back. He regarded them with rheumy eyes and said, 'I'm C.J. Chalmers, Sheriff of Cudahey County. You must be the ones who took Luther's pistol away from him.'

'That would be me,' Stone said. 'My friend there just watched.'

'Oh, so it just took one of you,' the sheriff said, nodding. 'Luther said a bunch of range hands jumped him.'

Mom laughed even louder, and the sheriff looked sour.

'Just the one,' Stone went on, straight-faced. 'My friend here is a lover, not a fighter. He leaves that stuff to me.'

Grady smiled at the sheriff proudly, nodding to affirm what Stone had said.

'What call did you have to jump my deputy?' the sheriff asked, in a hurt tone.

'He was exceeding his authority,' Stone snapped back. 'He was treating a couple of visitors to your town like suspects, without probable cause.'

44

The sheriff tried to explain, in a wheedling tone. 'Well now, Luther was just trying to stay on top of things, like I told him to. We like to head off trouble before it starts, keep out the troublemakers, if you know what I mean.'

Stone looked the sheriff in the eye. 'From what I've seen of this burg, you and your boys aren't having too much success, are you?'

The sheriff's mouth became a thin line and his eyes hardened. 'We got it about the way we like it. Rio Diablo is a nice town. It's a good place for a poor honest man to eke out a living. We just don't want any outsiders coming in here and rocking the boat. You know what I mean?'

Stone leaned back in his chair with a conciliatory smile. 'Look, Sheriff, I spent five years in law enforcement myself, so I know what you're up against.'

The sheriff's eyes narrowed when Stone mentioned his work in law enforcement.

Stone continued, 'My friend and I are visiting some old acquaintances in Rio Diablo, that's all. And as you can see, we're not carrying and not looking for trouble. In other words, don't push us and we won't push you.'

The sheriff smiled broadly. 'Well now, I see we understand each other. I'll tell Luther to forget about getting punched in the cods. Oh, by the way, I didn't catch your name.'

'Brimmer Stone, and this fellow is Grady Henderson, two travelers from Harris County visiting your fair city.'

Looking pleased with himself, the sheriff stood and picked up the old pistol from the table.

'Nice to make your acquaintance, fellows. Enjoy your visit. Stay out of trouble.' With those words, he walked out.

As the sheriff disappeared down the boardwalk, Stone said, 'I'll bet a double eagle that he's in the telegraph office in the next half-hour, asking Sheriff Baxter about us.'

'I'll bet along with you, Brim,' Grady said. 'I saw his face when you said you had been in law enforcement. Didn't like it a bit.'

Stone nodded at the door. 'If things around here are as corrupt as Barbara says they are, I'd imagine that the sheriff there doesn't want anyone looking over his shoulder.'

'Amen to that,' Mom cackled.

'So you know something about it, do you, Mom?' Stone asked.

'Why hell, yes,' she replied. 'Been around here since the Flood. That sheriff was elected by the citizens, but he works for Boss Bonner.'

'Who is Bonner?' Stone enquired.

Mom squinted her eyes as she groped her memory. 'He blew into town, musta been 'bout five years ago, nobody knows where from. Had plenty cash, and went into some kind of partnership with Sam Litchfield, who owned most of the saloons on California Street and a couple of fancy-houses out to Silver City. A couple of years ago, old Sam got hisself shot while riding home one night. Turns out that Bonner just happened to have a signed bill of sale for just about all of old Sam's property dated that same day. Claimed to have paid Sam in cash. The story was that Sam had the money on him when he got shot, and the high-wayman that done him in made off with it.'

'An odd coincidence,' Stone observed.

'Weren't it?' Mom shot back. 'Anyway, if you run a saloon round here, you rent your place and buy your whiskey from Boss Bonner. Those that don't end up with all kinds of trouble. They get a visit from those two strange boys, Smith and Jones.'

'What happened with the investigation of Litchfield's death? Anything?' Stone asked.

'Not a thing,' Mom grunted. 'His widow raised hell around here for a while, but she didn't have a thing on anybody. Boss Bonner, in his generosity, paid her way back east so she could go live with her sister, seeing as how she was almost stony broke.'

'Nice fellow. Does he bother you?' Brim wondered.

'Naw, I'm small potatoes,' she answered. ' 'Sides, I don't sell whiskey, so he don't even talk to me.'

The two paid Mom and thanked her for an interesting and informative morning, and promised her they would be back.

As they went out the door, Mom called, 'Careful about askin' questions. Smith and Jones might drop in for a visit.'

Back at the hotel, Grady confided to Stone that Jorene would be quitting work at The Garden of Eden and this would be her last night. He planned on spending the evening at the place, talking with Jorene while she wasn't working, and Stone was invited to come along.

'Barbara is going to be working late tonight, since it's Saturday,' Stone said. 'I suppose I can hang around with you for a while. It's probably a better place to kill time than in one of those saloons on California Street.'

That evening, Stone and Grady were in the parlor of The Garden of Eden. Grady was enjoying Jorene's company, and Stone was sampling the whiskey poured by Madam Ophelia's major domo, Shadrach.

'This is excellent whiskey, Shadrach,' Stone remarked.

'Yessir,' Shadrach agreed. 'Miz Ophelia special orders it. Otherwise, I'd be pouring a lesser quality liquor.'

'You don't get your whiskey from Boss Bonner?' Stone said.

Shadrach smiled broadly. 'You are learnin' about Rio Diablo already, Mr Brimmer.' Shadrach leaned close so he could whisper. 'Miz Ophelia says that the stuff Boss Bonner sells to everyone else in Rio Diablo is puma piss, if you'll pardon the expression. She flat turned him down after he ran off all the other wholesalers. Started ordering direct from a wholesaler in Fort Worth, has it shipped in by rail. I go down to the station and pick it up with my wagon. Makes it hard for anyone to hijack the load 'tween here and the station.'

'Are you telling me that someone has had a load of liquor hijacked?' Stone wanted to know.

'Yessir. Every wholesaler that tries to bring in a load by wagon mysteriously runs into highwaymen. Excepting, of course, Boss Bonner's wholesaler. You see, there's nothing but cotton fields 'tween here and Denton, about a thirty-mile stretch. A bunch of things can happen in thirty miles.'

Their conversation was interrupted by the arrival of a customer who caught Shadrach's eye. Stone turned to look at the man, and understood why he got Shadrach's attention. The man was tall, about six feet four, and cadaverously thin. He was dressed in a black coat, black hat, dark gray trousers and a white shirt with a string tie. But it was the man's face that riveted Stone's attention. The skin was so tightly stretched over high cheekbones and a jutting jaw that the face resembled a skull. When the man smiled, exposing his teeth, the illusion of a walking death's head was complete. Stone also noted the eyes. They were light gray and had the seemingly unfocused, faraway look that characterized, in Stone's experience, seriously disturbed people.

Even Madam Ophelia was taken aback by the man's appearance, but she quickly recovered her poise and enquired as to the man's pleasure. The man looked about the parlor carefully, until his eyes lit on Jorene sitting on a couch talking to Grady.

'That's the one,' the man said softly. 'The one in the yellow.'

'Excellent choice,' Madam Ophelia purred. Then she called to Jorene.

Jorene dutifully responded, after assuring an irritated-looking Grady that she wouldn't be long. As Jorene and the cadaverous man ascended the stairs to the second floor, Grady joined Stone at the bar. Shadrach poured Grady a drink, then, summoned by Madam Ophelia, assisted a tipsy elderly gentleman out to his horse.

Stone was telling Grady about what he had learned from Shadrach about the whiskey hijackings, when there was a scream from the second floor.

'That's Jorene!' Grady yelled, and ran for the stairs.

Stone made a grab for him but missed, calling, 'Grady, hold up!'

Stone started up the stairs after Grady, but was brushed aside by the burly Shadrach, who called, 'Stop, Mister Grady! Don't open the d—'

There was a shot on the second floor, followed by the sound of a body falling. Stone rushed up the stairs after Shadrach. When he reached the second floor, he could see Grady lying on his back in the hallway in front of an open door. Shadrach, with his pistol out, was cautiously peering into the room around the doorway. Jorene, nude from the waist up, screaming piteously, threw herself on Grady. As Stone reached Grady's side, there was a shot from within the room. Shadrach had fired once at someone outside on the ground.

Grady was conscious, and looking at Jorene questioningly. When Stone crouched to look at his wound, Henderson looked relieved and Brim recognized the look his friend always gave him when he arrived to help Grady out of a tight spot. He seemed to be saying, 'It's all right now, Brim's here.'

Stone immediately saw from the location of the wound that it was fatal. Grady looked at him hopefully, and his lips formed the word, 'Brim.' Then his last breath went out as a rattle and his eyes set.

As accustomed to death as Stone was, he was neverthe-less stunned. The person who had been his best friend for years was dead. He was only dimly aware of Jorene's pitiful sobs and her calling to Grady, as if she could call him back from the dead.

Shadrach came back to the doorway and said that he had missed his shot, that the pistol he carried in his shoulder holster on the job had too short a barrel for accuracy at that distance. He said that the shooter had a horse waiting in back, and rode off toward the creek bottoms.

With an effort, Stone tried to shake off the shock and sense of loss he was feeling. He told himself that the crime must be investigated immediately, and that he had to clear his mind. While waiting for the sheriff to appear, he got Jorene settled down enough to tell him what happened. Between sobs, she told him that the man had wanted to smoke a cigar and asked if he could open the window. When she said he could, he opened the window and lit his cigar. Then he asked her to undress so he could see her 'titties'. When she took off the top of her dress, he stuck his cigar on her left breast and that's when she screamed. Then he blew out the lantern and climbed out the window. The instant the door opened, he fired.

Stone went to the window and looked out. The back porch roof was directly under Jorene's window. One only had to climb out the window on to the roof, hang from the eave and drop to the ground. It was obvious to Stone that the place of the shooting had been carefully picked.

Stone took Shadrach aside. 'Shadrach, when one of the girls calls for help, or screams like tonight, is it your job to see about it?'

'Yessir. It's my job to take care of problems.'

'So it should have been you who opened the door to Jorene's room?'

'Yessir. 'Cept I don't throw open a door and make myself a target.'

'I understand. There are some things you know from experience.'

'Yessir. That's why I tried to call to Mister Grady not to go up there.'

Stone looked back at Grady's body, now covered with a sheet. 'The question is, Shadrach, why did a hired shooter want to kill *you*?'

Shadrach's facial expression told Stone that the black man knew the answer, but he was not ready to divulge it. With a quizzical glance, Shadrach looked past Stone at someone standing in the hallway. Stone turned to see that it was Madam Ophelia.

'Do *you* know why, Madam Ophelia?' Stone asked.

She was about to answer, when there were loud voices in the parlor.

'That's the sheriff,' she said. 'We'll talk after he's gone.'

CHAPTER 5

The sun was out, but it was a cool day. Stone thought grimly that since he had to bury his best friend, at least he had a decent day for it. There was one bunch of flowers on the coffin, which the whores from Madam Ophelia's place had brought. Stone couldn't find a local preacher who would have anything to do with a funeral for a range hand who had been shot to death in a whorehouse, so an itinerant Unitarian minister who was staying at the Cowboys' Rest agreed to say the words for the price of one night's lodging. He gave a short little sermon and said all the nice words he could for someone he had never met.

Jorene was inconsolable. Dressed in somber black, she sobbed by the grave supported by Madam Ophelia and one of the other girls from the Garden. Madam Ophelia herself was clad in black and silver, with a touch of scarlet at the neck. Four of Ophelia's other girls were there to offer moral support. Barbara, in mourning clothes and black veil, stood by Stone. She hadn't known Grady very well, but she saw the impact that his death had on Stone and so she had come to lend him her support. She had rarely seen any of Silver City's denizens up close and as the minister droned on, she surveyed them with curiosity.

After the short service was over and the others had gone, Stone waited until the gravedigger filled in the grave, then he paid him. The solemn man acknowledged Stone's payment with a tip of his hat, and walked away.

Stone knelt by the mound of earth.

'Well, *compadre*,' he said, 'I'm sorry I couldn't throw you a rope and pull you out of this one, but it all happened too fast. But you got your wish. You aren't buried by the side of the trail, out in the middle of nowhere, and your family, which I suppose is just Jorene and me, was here to mourn you. I'm going to get you a gravestone, so you won't be forgotten. And I promise you that by all that's holy or unholy, I'm going to get the son of a bitch that shot you.'

With that, Stone stood up, put his hat on and turned to Barbara. 'I appreciate your being here with me. It was good of you. I need to take you back home now, because I've got some work to do.'

'I understand,' she said, putting her hand on his arm. 'But don't get yourself killed while you're doing it. I've sort of taken a liking to you. When you finish up, come by.'

After driving Barbara home on her buckboard, Stone retrieved his horse and rode back to his hotel, where he picked up Grady's saddle-bags, then he rode out to Silver City. When he walked into The Garden of Eden, the place was empty except for Shadrach, who was behind the bar, polishing glasses.

'Shall I get Madam Ophelia for you?' he offered.

Stone put Grady's saddle-bags on the bar. 'Yes,' he replied. 'But first I need to see Jorene, if she's feeling up to it. I have some personal things of Grady's that I thought she might like to have.'

Shadrach smiled broadly. 'That's very decent of you, Mister Brim. I'll be right back.'

Shadrach escorted a shaken Jorene down the stairs and seated her at a table. Stone sat down across from her with the saddle-bags, and explained to her that Grady had carried some things around with him wherever he went and they meant something to him, and since he had no living relatives, the things should be hers. The tears started from her eyes as she looked at the worn saddle-bags and she reached out and stroked one of them gently. Then Stone gave her an envelope containing all the money Grady had to his name and had intended to use for setting up housekeeping. Jorene broke down and sobbed helplessly, and after a few minutes, Shadrach escorted her back up the stairs to her room.

When Madam Ophelia came down the stairs on Shadrach's arm, she had changed from her funeral clothes into a tasteful dressing-gown. She motioned to a table, and the three of them sat down. Shadrach poured a shot of bourbon for Ophelia and when Stone nodded in response to his unspoken question, he poured one for him, too.

Madam Ophelia spoke first. 'Mr Stone, you wanted to know who might want to kill Shadrach. We think we know, but it's rather complicated. Perhaps it will be better if I start, not at the real beginning, but where I think our current troubles started.'

Stone leaned back and sipped at his whiskey.

'Take your time,' he said. 'I've found it helps to start at the beginning.'

Madam Ophelia related the entire story about the death of Martin Duke in her kitchen ten days earlier, the hasty arrival of Sheriff C.J. Chalmers, his hurried search of Duke's person without confirming that the man was dead, and the newspaper clipping she had concealed from the sheriff.

'Do you still have the clipping?' Stone asked.

'Right here,' Ophelia told him, producing a prayer book from her pocket. The clipping was folded inside. 'It's dated 28 September 1880, five years ago.'

Stone spread it out on the table and started to read. As

54

he read, he said, 'Didn't you say the man who died in your kitchen was named Duke?'

'Yes. From his age, I figure he was the missing girl's father.'

'You take it from what this Duke fellow said that he saw Morley here in Rio Diablo?'

'He was dying at the time, and I could barely hear him,' Ophelia replied, 'but I've thought about it a thousand times, and I'm pretty sure what I told you was what he said.' She stood up and paced nervously. 'The only person in this town who has the weight to send the sheriff on a job like that one is Isaac Bonner.'

Stone nodded. 'I've heard of Bonner from a couple of sources. Neither was too complimentary. I understand he has the sheriff in his hip pocket.'

Ophelia smiled. 'That's one way of putting it. If Bonner stopped too fast, Chalmers would run right up his ass. But all that aside, I got crossways with Bonner before I opened my doors here. He came to call and let me know that he provided all kinds of services to business owners like myself. Among other things, he wholesaled whiskey, and wanted to take care of my needs. Well, I tasted that puma piss he passes off as whiskey, and I wasn't interested and told him so. He pointed out that whiskey wholesalers didn't have too much luck getting shipments into Rio Diablo, but I told him I'd worry about that.

'On top of that, he owned a Chinese laundry that he said could handle our laundry for us. Of course, in this business you use a lot of towels and sheets, and you need them laundered on a reasonably fast basis so you don't have to invest in too big an inventory. As far as the laundry went, I had a deal with Wong How's laundry to do the towels for five cents a dozen cheaper than Bonner's laundry would do them. That really riled Bonner, and it was only three days later that Wong How's place burned down.

'I started ordering my bar stock direct from a whole-saler in Fort Worth by telegraph, and he loads it on the train that runs from Fort Worth through here up into the territory. Shadrach picks up the load, always in daylight mind you, and brings it through town. Since Bonner couldn't figure out how to hijack our whiskey in broad daylight, he sent a couple of his cowboys to work over Shadrach. That was a serious miscalculation, because Shadrach is as good an eye-gouger, cheek-ripper and bone-breaker as you've seen anywhere in Texas and the Oklahoma Territory. When those two jumped him one night out back, Shadrach jacked 'em out so damned bad they ended up under a doctor's care. When they recovered enough to walk, they left town. So you can understand why Bonner doesn't like either one of us.'

Stone listened to the narrative in silence, but when Madam Ophelia finished her narrative, he asked, 'How long ago was it when Shadrach beat up the two bullyboys?'

Madam Ophelia thought for moment. 'Must have been about three years ago, wasn't it, Shadrach?'

'Yes, ma'am,' Shadrach responded. 'Close on to that.'

Stone frowned. 'Bonner wouldn't wait three years to get back at you. How long have those two dandy fellows that work for him now been around?'

'I think they showed up about a year ago, two peas in a pod,' Ophelia said.

Stone nodded. 'And they haven't bothered you?'

'Not in the least,' she replied, and Shadrach shook his head.

'It sounds more and more like this clipping is the connection, Ophelia,' Stone mused. 'Bonner is this embezzler, or he is close friends with him.'

Stone held up the clipping. 'Does this look like your Mr Bonner?'

'Hell,' Ophelia said. 'Cut off that beard and mustache,

56

and that could be your grandmother.'

Stone leaned back in his chair. 'We have to start with what we know. We know what the killer looks like, and that he probably was hired. What else do we know?'

'I think I have something,' Shadrach offered. 'When I took my shot at that killer as he was riding off, I saw a young'un running away. The killer had hired the boy to hold the horse because there's no hitching post out in back.'

'You sound like you're sure,' Stone said.

'I am,' Shadrach answered. 'I rounded him up today. Picked him up after the funeral. Thought maybe you'd want to talk to him. He's out in the kitchen eating a piece of Aunt Josie's apple pie. His name is Newt.'

'Newt!' Stone exclaimed. 'He gets around.'

When Shadrach brought Newt into the parlor, the boy was nervous and his blue eyes were wide with apprehension.

'I ain't goin' to get in no trouble, am I?' he asked, looking at Stone nervously. 'I din't know that feller was goin' to shoot nobody.'

'No, you're not in trouble,' Stone assured him. 'We just want to know what you know about that fellow.'

Somewhat reassured, Newt started to talk. 'Well sir, the first time I saw 'im, he ast me whar the livery stable was, and I told 'm. The second time I saw 'im, he ast me to hold his horse for 'im—'

Stone interrupted him. 'Where were you when he asked you about the livery stable?'

'At the depot.'

'When was that?'

'That morning, the morning before the shootin' that night.'

'The man came in on the train?'

'Yessir. The 9.45 from Fort Worth.'

'Then he went to the stable and rented a horse?'

'Yessir. I reckon it war the same'un that I helt that night for 'im.'

'Where did he go, when he rode away after the shooting?'

'I reckon he met somebody, 'cause he tole me to wait a while after he left, then get the horse on the other side of the Elm Creek bridge. And I did, and I took it back to the stable. He gimme a whole dollar to do that for 'im.'

'So he met somebody by the Elm Creek bridge and left, and you got the horse and returned it to the stable?'

'Thas right,' Newt declared proudly.

Stone gave Newt a two-bit piece and dismissed him. Newt left The Garden of Eden and trotted back toward town.

Stone looked at Madam Ophelia with raised eyebrows. 'I'm betting that the shooter was hired to get rid of Shadrach so there would be no trouble getting to you, Miss Ophelia. I think you were the final target in this. So we need to know who hired the killer, and there's only one way to find out. Looks like I'm going to Fort Worth.'

Ophelia nodded. 'And I'm going to pay your expenses, Stone. Nobody is going to shoot somebody in my place and get away with it. Find out who did the hiring, then I don't care what you do with the shooter. Bring him back here or blow his damned brains out. Either one is all right by me.'

When Stone left The Garden of Eden, he rode slowly back toward town, passing in front of The Erotica. The Erotica, which boasted a large front porch, sat directly across the street from The Garden of Eden. As Stone rode past, he noticed two men sitting on the porch at a small table that held two glasses. Stone recognized one of the men as one he had seen in front of the Lone Star saloon. The other, an overweight, florid-faced man, Stone took to be Mush Bourland, proprietor of The Eroticia. Both men watched him intently as he rode past, and he returned their gazes, nodding politely.

When Stone rang the bell at the Carrington house that night, the maid, a pleasant-looking gray-haired lady, opened the door.

'You must be Mr Stone,' she said cheerily. 'Please come in. I'm Bessie.'

'Hello, Bessie,' Stone said, handing her his hat and jacket.

Bessie hung up the hat and jacket, and said, 'Miss Carrington is waiting for you in the parlor.'

She led Stone into the parlor, where Barbara was sitting on the couch in front of the fire. 'Mr Stone, ma'am,' Bessie announced.

'Thank you, Bessie,' Barbara said. 'That will be all. Goodnight.'

Bessie nodded and, smiling, said, 'Goodnight, Miss,' then went out and closed the door.

Barbara rose. She was wearing a dark blue dressing-gown. When Stone kissed her, he could feel the heat from the fireplace on her skin and the gown. She wore a subtle scent, and the fragrance clung close to her body.

'Did you finish your business?' she asked, looking into his eyes.

'Just getting started. I'm leaving for Fort Worth tomorrow. I'm going after the hired gun that killed Grady. We believe he's the key to a lot more as well.'

After he explained what he had learned, he went to the table behind the couch and poured himself a drink from the decanter.

'Then you need to relax tonight, and forget about everything until tomorrow,' Barbara said softly.

Stone felt his fatigue melting away. He tossed down the

drink, put the glass on the table and slipped his arms around her waist.

She looked directly into his eyes. 'I don't know what you've done, Stone,' she said. 'I feel like you are the first real man that's set foot in this town in my memory. I could hardly wait till you got here tonight. I feel like a schoolgirl with a crush. But I shouldn't tell you that, should I? After all, you're just a man, and like all of them you think you're God's gift and your head will swell some more,' she whispered languidly.

Her words warmed him. The grief and the anger started to fade in that warmth.

She moved close to him and he held her, reveling in the heat of her body. 'I'm just like any man in that I want to hear a beautiful woman say I'm the only one that counts,' he said in a low voice. 'That's better than being told that you're handsome, brave or even smart.'

She put her arms around his neck, looking into his eyes questioningly.

'But how do you feel about me?' she said.

'Do you have to ask?' he replied, pulling her body closer to his, kissing her roughly. She responded eagerly. When the kiss ended, she turned and, holding him by the hand, led him to her bedroom.

Stone let himself melt into the heat of her passion, and the cares and thoughts of the day faded away.

CHAPTER 6

What would have been a hard two-day horseback ride to Fort Worth took three hours by train. Anticipating a short stay, Stone carried a small bag. At the Fort Worth depot, he was directed to a livery stable, where he rented a gentle buckskin mare. The mare handled nicely, and Stone had a leisurely ride to the sheriff's office.

When he was shown into the office of Sheriff Sloan, he introduced himself and said that he needed some help.

The sheriff looked at him for a moment, then said, 'Stone, Brimmer Stone. You were working in Harris County, weren't you?'

'That's correct, Sheriff,' Stone answered, somewhat surprised. 'However, I am no longer employed there.'

The sheriff smiled. 'That's what I understand. A Texas Ranger, name of Horn, was through here a couple of days ago, and told me about it. That's why I recognized your name. The way he told it, you got a royal screwing.'

'That's the way I feel about it, Sheriff.'

The sheriff leaned forward. 'Looking for a job, are you?' he asked expectantly.

'Not at the moment, Sheriff. Right now I'm looking for someone who I have reason to believe is from these parts.'

Disappointed, the sheriff leaned back and said, 'Too bad. From what I hear, you're a good man. "Bring 'Em

61

Back Alive Stone" he called you. I can always use a deputy who has his wits about him.'

'I appreciate that, Sheriff, and I may consider it one of these days. But right now, I have some business in Rio Diablo I've got to clean up.'

'Who is this you're looking for?' the sheriff asked.

'A hired gun,' Stone said, then started to describe the man. He was half-way through the description when he saw a look of recognition pass over the sheriff's face.

When Stone finished his description, the sheriff said, 'There's only one person in the world that looks like that, thank God. He's a local, all right. He's originally from a little town outside Fort Worth called Saginaw. His name is Eldritch. We've handled him a dozen times for everything from assault to suspicion of murder. He has served some time for minor stuff but we've never been able to get him for one of the big ones. He has an attorney and supporters that turn out alibis like hot cakes.'

'You know him as a hired gun?' Stone asked.

'Yep, and more. He enjoys using a knife. He carries a knife with a serpentine blade, which he stole when he was about sixteen. But he'll use a gun when he has to.'

'You say he can be found in Saginaw?'

'That's where he lives. However, I wouldn't recommend going out there. What you should do is talk to Gotcheye Priddy. Priddy is a contact for Eldritch.'

'Gotcheye Priddy?' Stone repeated, chuckling. 'I take it he has a bad eye?'

'Bad ain't the word for it,' the sheriff laughed. 'Several years ago, he and his girl, called Porky Sal, got into an argument while she was cooking his dinner. Seems that he was taking her whoring money and was spending it on another girl, named Bunty Kate. Old Sal grabbed a coring knife and tried to core out old Priddy's left eye. She damn near finished the job, before he brained her with a frying pan. He still has the eye, but it stares up and to the left all the time, like he's looking at someone behind you. It ain't a pretty sight.'

Stone chuckled. 'Where can I find old Gotcheye?'

Sloan turned to a map of the city, covering one wall of his office. 'He runs a saloon and whorehouse down in the Trinity River bottoms. Rough neighborhood. Take the main street to the east until you can't go any further, then turn north. This will put you on River Street.Priddy's place is about a half-mile down, called the Bangalore. Ugly place, you can't miss it. If you ask about Eldritch, he'll end up by finding you. So watch your back. By the way, who did he kill up in Rio Diablo?'

'My best friend,' Stone answered.

'I see,' said the sheriff, frowning. 'If you have to shoot the son of a bitch, make sure it's self-defense. But I'd hell of a lot rather you brought him in alive, you've got something that will stick.'

'I understand,' Stone replied.

As Stone left the main street and headed into the Trinity bottoms, he stopped and got his gunbelt and slung-shot out of his bag. He strapped on the gun, and put the billy in his right rear pocket. The mare soon carried him to the Bangalore, a shoddy structure backing up to the river. Stone wondered how many cowboys or drifters had gone in the front door of the place, but had been carried out the back and dumped in the river.

Stone walked in the front door and paused to let his eyes adjust to the darkness. The place reeked of whiskey, stale beer, river water and tobacco smoke. The bar was on the right, and the bartender with an ugly cocked eye fitted the description of the unattractive Priddy. A few customers were scattered about the room, staring at Stone as if he had just arrived from another world. Two gaudily dressed slatterns were leaning on the bar, appraising him with bloodshot eyes. As he approached the bar, one of them said, 'Hey there, gorgeous, looking for action?' She was missing a tooth from her upper gum, and her careworn face spoke volumes about a life lived the hard way.

'Not today, ma'am,' Stone answered politely. 'I'm here to talk to Mr Priddy.'

The two prostitutes looked disappointed and bored. They walked away.

'What can I do fer ya?' enquired Priddy, looking curious.

'Let me have a whiskey,' Stone said, eyeing the bottles behind the bar. 'The good stuff,' he added.

Priddy grinned and put down the bottle of cheap bourbon that he had been about to pour. He set a glass down in front of Stone and reached at the back of the regular stock, pulling out a nearly full bottle. He poured a shot.

'Twenty cents,' he said.

Stone tossed some coins on the bar and raised the glass to his nose, smelling it cautiously. Satisfied, he tossed the whiskey down and set the glass back on the bar.

Priddy waited for Stone to speak.

'Looking for a fellow named Eldritch. Understand you may know where he is.'

'Well, I might,' Priddy said. 'Comes and goes. Hard to nail down.'

When Priddy looked at him, Stone had to resist an urge to look over his own right shoulder.

'Why are you looking for Eldritch?' Priddy wanted to know.

'I have reason to believe he has some information that I need,' Stone replied.

'What kind of information?' Priddy asked, knitting his brow.

'Well now, that would be between me and Mr Eldritch,' Stone answered.

'You a lawman?'

'Nope.'

One of Priddy's patrons had walked up to the bar and was staring at Stone. He was a burly man with a lantern jaw, matted hair and filthy clothes. His stink surrounded him for six feet in all directions.

'Well, he looks like goddamn lawman to me,' the filthy man said, liquor slurring his words.

'Now, Ossie,' Priddy said, 'the man is minding his own business.'

'Well, my business is kickin' shit out of lawmen,' Ossie bellowed.

With that, he rushed at Stone, his right arm drawn back. Stone threw a straight right to his jaw, stopping the man in his tracks. Ossie looked surprised, then crumpled to the floor.

'Yew kain't do that to my friend!' another patron cried, rushing toward Stone.

Stone's hand was aching from contact with Ossie's jaw, so he pulled the billy from his rear pocket. As the man flailed wildly with his fists, Stone brought the billy down on top of his head. The assailant joined his friend Ossie on the floor.

Priddy had watched the whole thing disinterestedly from behind the bar. Stone turned to him and said, 'I don't care for the entertainment you put on here.'

'I don't either, and besides, it didn't last very long,' Priddy replied. Leaning over the bar to look at the two men on the floor, he said, 'Damn! If you keep knockin' out my customers, I'll have to close up. Why don't you find someplace else to go?'

'Tell me where I can find Eldritch,' Stone said coldly.

'I dunno,' Priddy answered. 'Ain't seen 'im. Maybe you better try tomorrow.'

'I'll be back tomorrow,' Stone said, and walked out.

Stone had ridden for two blocks when he glanced back and saw another horseman. When he reached midtown, the horseman was still there, keeping a safe distance. Stone smiled and spoke to the mare. 'If they'd asked me, I would have told 'em where I'm staying.'

Stone rode to the north side of town and pulled up in front of the Stockyards Hotel. He went in and took a room on the second floor, then saw to his horse, putting her up in the stable next door.

When he returned from the stable, Stone set about exploring the hotel. At the end of the hall, there was an emergency exit to a stairway that opened on to an alley at the rear of the hotel. The door could be opened from the inside, but not the stairway side. By experimenting, Stone found that a .45 cartridge placed in the striker plate receptacle prevented the latch from locking when the door was closed.

Back in his room, he examined the room key. In his bag, he had a ring of keys, which he compared to the room key one at a time. Finding a close match, he tried it in the door and found that his key worked admirably in the hotel's lock.

He descended to the lobby and told the desk-clerk that he would need a carriage at seven o'clock. Stone explained that he had an appointment for dinner with a lady on the south side of town and didn't want to get his horse out of the stable again. The desk clerk said he would have a carriage and driver waiting at the specified time. Stone noticed a nondescript man sitting in the lobby near the desk, who pretended to be reading a newspaper. Stone climbed the stairway to the second floor, but upon reaching the second floor hallway, he quietly retraced his steps and peered into the lobby. The man with the newspaper had abandoned his reading material and was hastening out of the hotel.

At seven o'clock, Stone left his room and locked it. He walked to the end of the hall and inserted a .45 cartridge into the striker of the emergency exit door, then walked downstairs to the lobby, where he turned in his key. The carriage was waiting as arranged, and Stone climbed aboard, telling the driver he was going to the south side and he would give directions as they went. The driver clicked his tongue to set the horse in motion, and they pulled away from the hotel and headed south.

Two blocks away, Stone had the driver turn right and then right again at the next street, and they headed back toward the hotel. Stone directed the driver in a circuitous route that took them to the alley at the back of the hotel. Stone told the driver to wait, tipped him generously, then entered the hotel by way of the emergency stairway. At the second floor, he pulled the door open and removed the cartridge. He moved quickly down the corridor to his room, and unlocked it with his own key. Relocking the door, Stone sat in the darkness in the room's only chair to wait.

Stone's patience was rewarded when, at eight o'clock, a shadow appeared under the bottom of the door and there was the noise of a key in a lock. Stone got up silently and flattened himself against the wall by the door, the billy in his hand. The door opened and a tall man stepped into the room. Stone took one step and struck the man in the back of the head. Stunned, the intruder fell to the floor. Stone quickly removed the man's weapons from their hiding places: a double action .38 revolver from a shoulder holster, a knife with an eight-inch serpentine blade from under the other shoulder, and a derringer from a leg holster. Putting the weapons aside, Stone lit the room's gaslight just as the man started stirring. The man felt the back of his head, then quickly went to his shoulder holster. Finding it empty, he slowly turned over to see who was holding him captive.

'Hello, Eldritch,' Stone said. 'I figured you for an ambush. You were going to wait until I opened the door, then you would have fired. Right?'

'You're a sly sum bitch, ain't ye?' Eldritch muttered. 'What do you want with me, cowboy?'

'To go back to Rio Diablo with me, to face charges for killing Grady Henderson,' Stone said, without emotion.

A look of realization passed over Eldritch's face. 'Oh, you mean that dumbass cowboy that stuck his nose in? Heard about that later on. Shoulda been the yellow boy.'

'That's what I figured. Who hired you?'

Eldritch pulled a wry face. 'Oh, come on, Stone. I ain't going to tell you shit.'

'I've got all night, Eldritch. And I figure that if I shoot off your fingers and toes one at a time, you'll decide to talk.'

Eldritch was indignant. 'Law officers can't do that.'

'I'm no law officer, my friend, I don't give a shit about the law. I'm working on my own. That fellow you killed was my partner. So it's six of one and a half-dozen of another whether or not you live to get back to Rio Diablo. Personally, I'd rather get shed of you early on, than have to wrestle you back sixty miles on that train. So, one way or another, you're going to pay.'

Eldritch was starting to lose his cockiness. The death's head grin began to fade.

'Who hired you to kill Shadrach?'

'Go to hell!'

Stone reached over and slapped the man on the side of the head with his billy, then turned him over on his stomach and pulled his hands behind him, clamping his wrists in manacles. Taking the knife off the table, he said, 'Let's see how this does in taking off finger joints.' Grabbing Eldritch's right hand, he pulled the index finger out straight.

'Let's try the trigger finger to start.'

Stone began to apply pressure with the blade's edge against the finger's first joint.

'No, no, no! Hell, I'll tell you who it was.'

Stone kept applying the pressure till Eldritch started squealing. 'All right, I'll tell you, just don't cut.'

'Give me a name,' Stone demanded.

'Mush Bourland,' Eldritch declared, almost yelling.

'The Mush Bourland that runs the Eroticia whorehouse?'

'Yes, that's him, now don't cut!'

'All right, you can keep your fingers,' Stone growled. 'But you and me are going for a little ride.'

'Where to?'

'We're taking a carriage ride down to the depot, then we're taking the first train to Rio Diablo, ' Stone answered.

Eldritch was indignant. 'You sure are a cocky sum bitch!' he spat. 'How do you think you're gonna get me all the way to Rio Diablo?'

Stone lifted Eldritch to his feet and put the confiscated weapons in his bag. Holding the manacles by the chain, Stone pushed Eldritch down the hall to the emergency door and down the steps. Stone pushed open the door at the bottom of the stairs and peered out. In the darkness of the alley, he could make out the horse and carriage where he had left it. He pushed Eldritch out the door toward the carriage.

Suddenly, Stone saw that something wasn't right. The carriage driver was silhouetted by a gaslight at the end of the alley, and appeared to be a large, heavy man. Stone's driver had been a tall, thin man, almost gangling. He heard a step behind him and he realized that he had underestimated his quarry.

CHAPTER 7

Stone ducked, spun to his right and felt the manacle chain slip out of his hand. The iron pipe that was intended to cave in his head, struck his shoulder with a glancing blow. He threw an upper cut at the shadow holding the pipe. The blow missed the chin, but hit the assailant's throat. The pipe-wielder made a grunting sound and grabbed his throat, dropping the pipe. Stone drew his Colt and fired point-blank into the man's body.

Eldritch dove under the horse and rolled on to his back. Folding his knees into his chest, he slipped the manacle chain under his feet and jumped erect. The man on the carriage tossed a pistol to him then fired at Stone. Stone heard the slug whistle by his head and ricochet off the side of the building. Before the man could cock his six-shooter again, Stone fired twice at his silhouette and the stocky man fell over the back of the coachman's seat.

Eldritch crouched and fired under the horse's belly at Stone's feet. Stone felt an impact on his right boot and a burning sensation in his shin. The horse, spooked by the shots, reared, and Stone dropped flat on his stomach. The panicked horse dashed forward down the alley, exposing Eldritch. In the split second before Eldritch realized that Stone was on the ground instead of standing, Stone had fired twice. Eldritch dropped the pistol and staggered backward, trying desperately to stay on his feet. He stumbled into the wall of the building siding the alley, staring at Stone. Two dark patches appeared on his shirt, where Stone's shots had penetrated his chest.

Stone said, 'That's for Grady, you son of a bitch.'

Eldritch's mouth worked open and shut three times as if he were trying to speak and his lips drew back from his teeth in a grotesque grimace. Then his knees buckled and he slid down the wall and fell sideways, with his face in the alley's muck.

The terrified horse and the carriage rattled out of the alley, and there was a dead silence. Stone checked Eldritch for a pulse, and found none. He unlocked the manacles and returned them to his bag. He then looked at the man who had tried to brain him with the pipe. The man lay on his back, eyes open as if he had been surprised. Again there was no pulse. Stone recognized the man as Ossie's friend from Priddy's saloon, and he realized that the stocky man on the carriage probably had been Ossie himself. He made a mental note to revisit Priddy. But then, he thought, living and looking like he does is probably the worst punishment for Priddy anyway.

Stone looked around the alley and saw what looked like a bundle of clothes twenty-five feet down the alley. He found the frail carriage driver bleeding from a wound to his head, but still alive.

The hotel's back door opened and the desk clerk peered out cautiously. Stone shouted to him to call a doctor and the law. The clerk disappeared back inside.

After the doctor tended to the carriage driver, he checked Stone's ankle and found that, though the boot was ruined, the wound itself was minor, no more than a graze. Stone then spent the rest of the night with the deputies that showed up to investigate. They told him a couple of cowhands returning from a saloon down the street had stopped a runaway carriage and found a dead man in it, with two holes in his chest. Stone assured them that the corpse was part of the alley bunch. When they finished up at the scene, Stone accompanied them back to the sheriff's office.

Stone was drinking coffee when the sheriff arrived.

The sheriff looked at him quizzically. 'I thought you were supposed to bring 'em back alive,' he said softly. Then he shouted, 'Hell's fire, Stone! You left dead men all over north Fort Worth!'

'I tried to bring him in, Sheriff, but his friends had something else in mind,' Stone told him.

'Come on in here,' the sheriff said, pointing at his office.

The sheriff hung up his hat and said, 'The deputies gave me a rundown on what went on, and it looks like the shooting was justified. The fact that they koshed that carriage man shows they were setting up an ambush. The only question is, did you illegally detain Mr Eldritch against his will? If so, that's kidnapping.'

'Sheriff,' Stone said evenly, 'we were going someplace to talk things over and I ran into an ambush.'

'I looked at those bodies on my way here this morning,' the sheriff said. 'There are some strange bruises on Eldritch's wrists. You wouldn't know anything about that, would you?'

'It's a mystery to me,' Stone answered.

'That's what I thought. Stone, the way I look at it, the county is better off. Those two with Eldritch have been behind bars more than they been in front of 'em. So I'm goin' to accept my deputies report the way you told it to 'em, and forget about this whole thing.'

Stone smiled. 'That's mighty good of you, Sheriff. I feel that justice has been served and, like you say, the world, not to mention the county, is better off.' He rose to go. 'I'll be heading back to Rio Diablo. I found out enough that I've got some more work to do back there.'

'That's good,' the sheriff said. 'Just make sure you do it

in Cudahey County, this time. And one more thing, Stone.'

'What's that, Sheriff?'

The sheriff's tone was almost pleading. 'Please don't come back to Fort Worth anytime soon.'

Before boarding the train for the trip back to Rio Diablo, Stone sent a telegram to Madam Ophelia, telling her he had additional information and that Grady's murderer was dead.

Upon arriving at Rio Diablo, Stone collected his horse from the stable and sought out Newt.

'Newt, come with me. I may have a job for you,' Stone said.

Newt climbed on to the horse and sat behind Stone.

Back at The Garden of Eden, Stone had Newt stay with the horse while he went in and sat down with Madam Ophelia and Shadrach. When he said that Mush Bourland had hired Eldritch, both were surprised.

'We've never had a speck of trouble with Bourland,' Ophelia said. 'When I first opened up, he suggested a partnership to me and I turned him down. He didn't seem to be too upset over it and we haven't heard a peep out of him since.'

'Who does he answer to?' Stone asked.

'No one that I know of,' Ophelia answered. 'However, he's played Bonner's game since he's been running The Eroticia. If anyone has a grip on him, it would be Bonner. He buys Bonner's liquor, uses Bonner's laundry and pays Bonner rent on his building.'

Brim glanced outside. 'It's still early. I think I'll have a little visit with Mr Bourland.'

Stone strolled casually across Silver City to The Eroticia. When he walked in the front door, Big Sally, The Eroticia's madam, greeted him warmly.

'Well, big fellow, yer the early bird today, aintcha? You'll hafta wait a minute till I get the girls down here.'

'Don't bother, ma'am,' Stone said. 'I'm here to see Mr Bourland.'

Big Sally was disappointed. 'Oh, well,' she said. 'Cain't win 'em all. He's back inna office. Come this way. Whachur name?'

'Stone.'

The madam led Stone down a hall and rapped on the last door.

'Hey, Mush!' she called. 'Gent named Stone's here to see you.'

'Send him in,' came the reply.

Bourland was about fifty years old, five feet nine, with a waistline that revealed a disdain for physical activity. The puffiness of his face indicated that he was given to rich food and liquors, and he shook hands with Stone limply. It was rumored that Bourland had been a successful swindler in the deep south of his boyhood, after his family fell on hard times during reconstruction. His current profession of whorehouse-owner was a convenient hiding place from the law that sought him in other climes.

'What can I do for you, Mr Stone?' he asked amiably.

'Well, sir,' Stone started, 'I've been over in Tarrant County for a couple of days, and I ran into someone who said he knows you.'

Smiling, Bourland asked, 'Oh? Who's that?'

Stone, casually glancing around at the risqué art hung on the office walls, said, 'Tall fellow, name of Davis Eldritch.'

Bourland blinked once, swallowed hard and said, 'I'm sorry, but I don't recognize the name.'

'Well, like I said, he's a tall fellow, about six four, and skinny as all get out. Not very pretty, either. Face looks more like a skull than a proper face. Wears black all the time, with a black hat. Speaks in kind of a whisper. Sort of strikes you as an undertaker.'

Stone could see a film of perspiration forming on

Bourland's upper lip.

Bourland cleared his throat, then said, 'No, doesn't sound familiar. Are you sure he was talking about me?'

'Quite sure. Mentioned The Eroticia, in fact.'

Bourland dabbed at his forehead with a handkerchief and managed a weak smile. 'That explains it,' he said, sounding relieved. 'He was a customer, that's why I don't remember. Hundreds of fellows come through here. I meet some of them.'

'No, I don't think so,' Stone said quietly. 'I got the impression *you* were the customer, not him.'

Bourland forced a smile and rose to his feet. 'I'm sorry, I don't remember the fellow. Now, if you'll excuse me, I have an appointment downtown. If you see Eldritch again, give him my regrets.'

'Oh, I won't be seeing him again, I'm afraid,' Stone replied. 'He's dead.'

Bourland paled and seemed to sag. 'Dead? What happened to him?'

'I shot him through the heart and lungs with this,' Stone said calmly, patting the .45 at his hip.

Bourland sagged even more and reached out to his desk for support. Swallowing several times, Bourland finally croaked, 'Had a disagreement, did you?'

'You can call it that,' Stone answered. 'Pity you have to rush off. I'll come back tomorrow and we can talk some more.'

This time, Bourland's forced smile bordered on the grotesque. 'Yes, you do that,' he squeaked.

As Stone rose and walked out the door, Bourland was swabbing at the rivulets of sweat running down the back of his neck.

Stone walked back to The Garden, where Newt was waiting with the horse. 'Newt, you know how to ride a horse, don't you?'

'You betcha, Mr Stone,' Newt beamed. 'I's prackly raised in the saddle.'

'Good. You know Mr Bourland?'

'Sure.'

'I think he's going to leave his office in a few minutes, probably out the back door. I want you to cold-trail him and see where he goes. Don't let him see you.'

Delighted, Newt grabbed the saddlehorn and pulled himself up into the saddle. Stone went into The Garden and watched through the front window. After a few minutes, Bourland emerged from behind The Eroticia on his buckboard. Newt waited a few moments, then nudged his horse into a walk.

Inside, Stone said, 'I think if we wait a while, we will have some more information. Bourland was almost pissing in his pants when I left him. If I'm any judge of character, he's running for help right now.'

Ophelia laughed. 'I'm glad you're on our side, Stone.'

Stone turned to Shadrach. 'Shadrach, I think you have a bottle of brandy in your bar. I would highly appreciate a taste of it.'

'It's on the way,' Shadrach said, grinning.

Shadrach returned to his duties, preparing for the night's business, Ophelia went upstairs to change into her 'working clothes', and Stone had two brandies while they waited for Newt's return.

After an hour, Newt trotted up to the hitching rail in front of The Garden, tied up Stone's horse and ran to the front door. Ophelia, dressed in her evening finery, came down to hear Newt's report. He gave a sprightly narrative of his adventure, between sips of sarsaparilla supplied by Shadrach.

'I followed Mr Bourland downtown and he tied up his rig in front of the Lone Star saloon, and he seemed to be in a big hurry. He went up the stairs in the saloon to where Mr Bonner's office is.'

Stone and Ophelia exchanged glances.

'So I tied up your horse, Mr Stone, and went around to the back of the Lone Star. They's a shed at the back of the building with a low roof, and I clumb up on a pile of fire-wood to the roof of the shed and snuck up to Mr Bonner's back window, the one with the bars. I stayed low so they wouldn't see me, and I laid there and listened. Boy hidy, that Mr Bonner was some angry with Mr Bourland. I couldn't make out all what was said but Mr Bonner called Mr Bourland a bunch of bad names includin' "a hysterical old woman".'

'I had Bourland figured right, it looks like,' Stone said.

Newt went on. 'When Mr Bonner got through chewing on Mr Bourland's backside, he tol' him to go back to his "crab palace" and get back to work. That's when I unclimbed that roof and came on back.'

Stone reached into his pocket and pulled out a handful of coins which he handed to the boy. 'You've done a good day's work, son, more than I had any right to expect,' he said.

Newt beamed happily and finished off the last of his drink.

'Wait outside, Newt,' Stone instructed.

After the boy had gone out, Stone said, 'It's no surprise. Bonner got Bourland to do the contracting for him so he would stay clean. I'm going back to see Bourland tomorrow. Maybe I can crack him. The problem is, what do we do if Bourland confesses? There's every indication that Sheriff Chalmers is in Bonner's hip pocket, so taking him to the local law is a waste of time. We are going to have to act on our own, and it could get bloody. Are you two up for that?'

'The way I look at it,' Ophelia said, 'it can't get any more dangerous for me than it is right now. I can't speak for Shadrach.'

Shadrach said, 'They already sent one killer after me. I

reckon I'll just have to hang on till somebody wins.'

'That's it, then,' Stone said. 'I'm just about asleep on my feet and, I'm going back to the hotel. Bright and early in the morning, I go to see Bourland and jerk his traces a little more.'

Stone, with Newt aboard, rode back to the hotel, had a light supper in the dining-room, and wasted no time in getting into bed.

He was sound asleep at midnight, when there was a knock on his door. Instantly he was awake and on his feet, the .45 in his hand. He flattened himself against the wall by the door and called out, 'Who's there?'

The reply came from the hallway, 'Stone, my name is Jones. I work for Mr Isaac Bonner. He wants to talk to you.'

'In the middle of the night?' Stone growled.

'Mr Bonner told me to apologize for getting you out of bed. He feels that it's important to talk to you tonight.'

'You alone?' Stone asked.

'Yes sir, I am. And unarmed.'

Stone unlocked the door and eased it open enough to stick the barrel of the .45 out through the crack, aimed at the midsection of his visitor. The visitor raised his hands and turned around slowly, so that Stone could see he was not carrying. The man was wearing sharply creased trousers, polished boots and an expensive shirt. Stone recognized him as Smith's two-gun friend he had seen on the boardwalk in front of the Lone Star saloon.

Stone opened the door, motioned the man inside and lit his lamp.

'Now that I'm awake,' Stone said grumpily, 'I might as well go see what your Mr Bonner has to say. But what's so damned important it won't wait till morning?'

Smirking, Jones replied, 'Mr Bonner figures anything he wants to do is important.'

Stone returned the smirk. 'By God, it better be.'

CHAPTER 8

Jones had a buckboard outside, and they quickly covered the short distance to the Lone Star. The saloon was deserted, except for a janitor sweeping the floor. Jones led Stone through the main room to the stairs. Bonner's office was on the second floor, at the rear of the building.

The office was well appointed and comfortable. The paneled walls suggested luxury, and a thick rug deadened the sound of boot heels. Tasteful paintings hung on three walls. Bonner sat cradled in a large padded armchair, behind an imposing mahogany desk. The room's only window was directly behind him. Bonner himself was unprepossessing, standing about five feet ten, with a tendency toward a spreading waist. He was clean-shaven, and his dark hair was graying at the temples and thinning over his forehead. His brown eyes were bright and piercing. Shaking his proffered hand, Stone noted that it was smooth and soft as a baby's.

Bonner cordially offered Stone a chair facing the desk, and asked if he'd like a cup of coffee. Stone said, 'Thank you, no', and turned to look at the room behind him. In the relative darkness at the back of the room, Jones sat with another man who was wearing a six-shooter on his belt. The other man was Smith.

Turning back to Bonner, Stone remarked, 'I don't care

for your seating arrangements, Mr Bonner. I'd rather your boys sat up here where I can see them, rather than have them staring at the nape of my neck.'

Bonner motioned to the two, and they moved their chairs beside Bonner, one on each side.

'There now, that's a lot better,' Stone said. He noticed that the men were dressed similarly, in expensive wool pants, flannel shirts and highly polished boots.

'You are a cautious man, Mr Stone,' Bonner said.

'Yes,' Stone replied. 'A cautious *live* one.'

Bonner chuckled. 'Where was that caution when you went up against three gunmen in Fort Worth yesterday?'

Stone smiled. 'The telegraph is a wonderful thing, isn't it?'

'Yes indeed,' Bonner said. 'I was waiting for a reply to my enquiry regarding the death of one Davis Eldritch before I sent for you, just in the way of confirmation, you understand, and imagine my surprise to learn that not only was Mr Eldritch quite dead, but so were two of his . . . ah, *associates.*'

'They were not cautious,' Stone said, with a half smile.

Bonner threw back his head and laughed. 'No, indeed.'

'Why am I here?' Stone asked.

Bonner leaned back in his chair and put his fingertips together as if about to pray. 'I am interested in you, Mr Stone. You have been a formidable lawman, but now have been "defrocked" shall we say, escaping the Harris County grand jury through a political maneuver. You are a skilful gunfighter, as attested by your success against Eldritch, perhaps the best cold-blooded killer that Tarrant County had to offer. And now you are at loose ends. What I'm talking about here is employment, Mr Stone, in a job for which you are uniquely suited. I know what you made as a deputy sheriff in Harris County and I am prepared to double that salary.'

Stone noticed that Smith and Jones exchanged quick glances.

'That's a very generous offer, Mr Bonner. Just what do I have to do to earn that salary?' Stone wondered.

'You would be a troubleshooter, something on the order of what Mr Smith and Mr Jones do now,' Bonner said, nodding at each of the men in turn.

'That would include getting people out of bed at midnight?' Stone asked.

Bonner chuckled. 'Yes indeed, among other things. Collecting debts, persuading business associates of the wisdom of my position during disputes, eliminating "obstacles", shall we say, to the smooth progress of my enterprises.'

'I see,' Stone said, glancing at the two flanking Bonner and noting that they didn't look pleased with the way the conversation was going. 'You have Smith and Jones here, and they look reasonably competent. Why do you need me?'

Bonner smiled. 'You have what we'll call unique quali-fications.' Rubbing his hands together, he said, 'What do you say, Mr Stone? Do we have a deal?'

Stone didn't like the odds of getting back to his hotel room if he said no, so he decided to hedge. 'Well, that's a big decision, Mr Bonner. It involves a change in the way I've been living and thinking. So I couldn't make a snap decision. I'll have to sleep on it.'

Impatience flickered over Bonner's face, but was quickly replaced by a toothy smile.

'Of course, yes indeed. One saves the snap decisions for the gunfight. This kind of decision requires reflection. I understand perfectly. How about in the morning?'

'Sure,' Stone answered, rising to his feet. Smith and Jones also rose.

'Mr Jones will take you back to your hotel,' Bonner said.

'Get a good night's sleep. Decisions are easier when you have a clear head.'

During the drive back to the hotel, Jones, now wearing two matched pistols, was silent. As they pulled up in front of the hotel, Stone asked, 'Do you like your job?'

'Why not?' Jones answered. 'The pay is good and nobody in town gives me any shit. I'm good at what I do,' he added, patting one of the pistols.

'Well, you can't beat that kind of recommendation,' Stone said, stepping down from the buckboard. 'Goodnight.'

Jones clicked his tongue at the horse and pulled away without speaking. Stone watched him pull away and wondered, if he were to take the job, how long Jones and his friend would let him live.

Stone returned to his room and got seven hours of uninterrupted sleep.

The next morning, Stone saddled his horse and rode to Silver City for a talk with Madam Ophelia. As he rode past The Eroticia, he changed his route enough to allow him a look at the back of The Eroticia. Bourland's buckboard was in its shed.

Ophelia was having her morning coffee when he walked in, and she invited him to sit down and have some breakfast. She called to Aunt Josie for another plate. After coffee was poured, Stone filled in Ophelia on his midnight visit.

'He obviously doesn't need me,' Stone said. 'Smith and Jones supply all the muscle he can use. His offer to me was because of my acquaintance with you.'

'Do you think it's because of the clipping?' Ophelia asked.

'I know of no other reason why he would hire a gunman to kill Shadrach. He needed a clear path to get to

82

you, and wanted it to look like the work of some kind of loco transient. You said that Sheriff Chalmers went through Duke's wallet first thing, even before he looked at the wound?'

'Yes, he did. I thought it was strange at the time. He didn't check for a heartbeat, try to identify the man or count the money in the wallet; he was looking for something, and he knew exactly what it was.'

Stone nodded. 'What I think happened was that Mr Duke finally tracked down his Mr Morley. The problem was that Morley saw him, and recognized him too. If Duke had been wandering around the country looking for Morley and showing that clipping to folks, chances are that Morley knew about it. Assuming that Morley and Bonner are the same person, he probably sent someone to kill Duke and get the clipping. Only things didn't go as planned, and Duke didn't go down when he was hit and he shot back at his killer. That's why he made it to your back door with the clipping still on him. Chalmers was instructed to find the clipping because the shooter didn't get it. He was either incompetent in his search, or so arrogant that your suspicions didn't matter to him. Then, since it was missing, they assumed that you had it. Bonner's offer to me was another way to get his hands on the clipping without arousing suspicion.'

Stone finished the last of his bacon and eggs, and stood up. 'Thanks for the breakfast. Now I think I'll wander on over to The Eroticia and pay Mr Bourland a visit.'

'Watch your step,' Ophelia warned.

When Stone walked in the front door, Big Sally was in a dressing-gown and curlers, puttering around in her parlor. When she saw Stone, her eyes widened and she looked distressed.

'Well, if it ain't Mr Stone,' she said, assuming a casual air. 'What can we do for ya today?'

'I need to have some chat with Mr Bourland,' Stone replied. 'We didn't finish our conversation yesterday.'

'Well, yer outta luck, mister. He ain't here. Hadda leave town on business, suddenlike. But I kin tell 'im you came calling.'

'That's a surprise, Sally,' Stone said. 'How'd he go? His buckboard is still here.'

Sally hesitated, then her eyes rolled up and to the left, avoiding Stone's stare. 'Ah, Willy took 'im to the depot this morning, he hadda take the train,' she muttered.

'Is that so? You won't mind if I just take a look in his office, would you?' Stone said, starting toward the hallway.

Big Sally tried to move her considerable bulk between Stone and the hallway, but he brushed by her. Sally moved into the hallway behind him, shouting, 'Mr Bourland ain't here, Mr Stone, like I told ya.'

Before he reached the office door, Stone heard another door close. He was certain it was Bourland's back door. He opened the hall door on to an empty office. The scent of fresh cigar smoke hung in the air.

'See thar, I told ya,' Sally said, with satisfaction.

'So you did,' Stone replied, smiling. He turned and, to Sally's relief, walked out the front door.

Stone walked back to the palace and found Ophelia in the parlor.

'Looks like Mr Bourland is avoiding me. I imagine it was Bonner's orders.'

'What's next?' Ophelia asked.

'I'll have to sneak up on him. In the meantime, I have some business downtown.'

'Wouldn't be in a millinery shop, would it?' she said, smiling.

'It might,' replied Stone. 'Been thinking about getting one of those new hats with the ostrich feathers.'

Ophelia threw back her head and laughed. 'You'd be

the sweetest thing in town, Stone.'

The Lone Star saloon's main room was deserted except for the bartender, who nodded to Stone as he walked through and took the stairway at the back of the room. At the top of the stairs, he stopped at the doorway and rapped three times. The murmur of a conversation on the other side stopped, and the door opened an inch or so. Smith peered out at him, then called, 'It's Stone.'

'Let him in,' Bonner replied.

As Stone walked in, Bonner stood behind his desk, smiling.

'Have a seat, Mr Stone,' he said, 'and how about some coffee?'

'Thank you, no,' Stone replied. 'I won't be staying long.'

The smile melted from Bonner's face.

'I just wanted to let you know,' Stone continued, 'that I won't be taking you up on your job offer.'

Bonner frowned, then smiled toothily. 'If it's money, I'm open to negotiation,' he purred.

'No, it's not the money,' Stone said. 'It's too much of a change for me. Instead of protecting the citizens, I'd be strong-arming them, knocking them around to keep them in line. I don't think I care for that.'

Bonner's face grew flushed as Stone talked. 'Too bad you see it that way, Mr Stone. That's unfortunate, yes indeed. I want you to know that, in Rio Diablo, if you're not with us, you're against us. Do you understand, Mr Stone? Don't stick your nose in where it shouldn't be. I suggest you make your own business your *only* business.'

Stone stared at Bonner eye to eye. 'When Eldritch gunned down my partner, a lot of things in this damned town became my business,' he said. 'Now, if you'll excuse me.'

He strode to the door and walked out, while Bonner

glared at his back.

Brimmer remounted and rode the two blocks to the millinery shop. He left his horse in front of the general store, and walked across the street to Barbara's shop.

When he walked in, a little bell over the door tinkled. There were no customers in the shop, and Barbara was alone.

Barbara looked up from what she was doing, and tried to look stern.

'Well, it's about time,' she said briskly. 'How did your trip go?'

'Got what I was after.'

'What about that man who shot Grady? What happened to him?'

'Well, let me put it this way; he won't be shooting any more cowboys.'

Barbara frowned. 'I don't think I want to ask why.'

'Good.'

'Why didn't you let me know you were back?'

'I've been tied up,' he answered. 'Some things had to be gotten out of the way before I could start enjoying myself.'

'What is it that was so important?'

'For one thing, I got a job offer and had to consider it.'

'A job offer? You mean honest work?'

'No, not exactly. It was working for Isaac Bonner.'

'My God! You didn't take it, did you?'

Stone laughed at her shocked tone. 'No, of course not. Have a little faith!'

'What did he want you to do?'

Brim shrugged. 'Muscle; intimidation; murder, probably.'

'That sounds about right, but I thought he had that strange pair of gunmen for that already.'

'He does. Besides, he was just trying to use me to get to

someone else. The way I figure it is that after I finished what he wanted me to do, I'd have ended up off the side of a road somewhere, with a bullet in my back.'

'I suppose he wasn't too happy when you turned him down.'

'I don't think so.'

'You're going to have to watch your back, Stone,' she said, a slight tremor in her voice.

'You sound like you care,' he said, reaching for her and pulling her close.

'Don't start that, Stone. A customer could walk in any minute,' she whispered.

He pulled her closer and kissed her a long, hard kiss. She didn't want to, but she responded and pressed her body to his.

When the kiss ended, she said, 'It's a slow day, and Milly isn't due back for a while. Let's get out of sight.'

They walked to the office area at the back of the store, then she turned and embraced him almost violently, pressing her lips to his. Her excitement grew, and she hungrily explored his mouth with her tongue.

Just then, the bell over the front door tinkled.

She called out, 'Just a moment,' and patted at her hair.

'Stay here,' she whispered, kissing Brim on the ear, then bustled out to greet her customer.

He waited only a few minutes till she returned.

'What do you say I take the rest of the day off, and we go to my house?' she suggested.

Stone grinned and said, 'Sounds like a good plan to me.'

Shortly, Milly appeared, and Barbara turned over care of the shop to her for the rest of the day. Barbara drove her buckboard home, while Stone rode beside her. At the house, Stone put his horse in Barbara's shed, fed him and bedded him down. He planned on a long and exhausting night.

CHAPTER 9

When Stone awoke the next morning, Barbara was already up. He slipped into his clothes and, guided by the aroma of freshly brewed coffee and frying bacon, found her in the kitchen.

'If I remember correctly,' she said, 'you like your eggs fried in butter, not bacon grease.'

'Good memory,' Stone remarked, as he poured himself a cup of coffee.

'And you have no objection to hot biscuits.'

'Right again.'

Soon, she placed a basket of biscuits in the center of the table, along with a pound of butter, and she followed these up with a plateful of over-easy eggs and crisp bacon.

As they ate, Stone said, 'The first night I was here, you mentioned the corruption in this town and something about the sheriff's office. Tell me about it.'

She thought for a moment, frowning. 'The town had always been a little rough, like all frontier towns. But things started getting more civilized as the farmers moved in and my daddy built the cotton gin. The last sheriff we had before C.J. Chalmers was Royce Simmons. He probably wasn't the best sheriff in the world, but basically he was honest. He spent most of his time trying to keep those Oklahoma cowboys under control, and keeping them away from the regular townspeople. His deputies were good men, and were more interested in protecting the regular folks than getting rich.

'The real problems started about four years ago, when Isaac Bonner showed up from out of nowhere. I think you heard about Litchfield, Bonner's partner, who got mysteriously killed right after signing away his property to Bonner. The next thing that happened was that Sheriff Simmons was shot in the back by 'assailant or assailants unknown', according to the coroner's jury. The county commissioners promoted the senior deputy, Boke Wallace, to replace him for the rest of his unexpired term. Everyone sort of took it for granted that Boke would run for sheriff when election time came. But the campaign had no sooner started than Boke withdrew his name, packed up, left town and moved to Denton County. He got a job as deputy over there. It surprised everyone in Rio Diablo, since he was considered a dead cinch to win the election.'

'Anyone ask him why?'

'Sure. But he wouldn't talk. He said something about it being time to move on, or something vague like that. And guess who the only candidate for sheriff was?'

'C.J. Chalmers.'

'He had money behind him. He took full pages in the newspaper to tell everyone how wonderful he was. Had posters all over the county asking people to vote for him. No one else had that kind of money to spend; he scared off everyone else that would have liked to have the job. And this is a person who was never a success at anything he tried, farming, running a store, working for someone else. Probably never had fifty dollars in his pocket at any one time in his life.'

'Did anyone wonder where the money came from?' Stone asked.

'Sure. Pretty soon the word got around that Isaac Bonner was backing Chalmers. It was kind of an open secret. Anyway, after the election, all the deputies quit and Chalmers brought in his own people, including his dimwit nephew.'

'I met the nephew,' Stone said, chuckling.

Barbara went on. 'That's when things started to change. It was subtle, but finally everyone got to noticing. Anybody that crossed Bonner would get into trouble with the law, or have some kind of accident. At first, the sheriff and his boys would think up some ordnance that was broken or some license that hadn't been bought, or some tax that hadn't been paid. Bonner tried to get Russ Ansley over at the general store to start selling whiskey and, of course, buy it wholesale from him. Ansley told him to go to hell and if he had any problems, he would go straight to the Attorney General in Austin. Since then, they leave him and the other legitimate merchants alone. But the people on the edge of the law, like the saloonkeepers and the people that run the houses out on Silver City, are fair game.'

'Has anyone contacted the Rangers?' Stone asked.

'Not that I know of,' Barbara replied.

'It looks like Isaac Bonner has a free hand in Rio Diablo.'

'I guess you can say that.'

Stone thought for a moment. 'There's something else.'

'Oh?'

'I have suspicions that Isaac Bonner may not be his real name. He may be a fugitive named Richard Morley, from Chicago. This Morley took a bunch of people for a hell of a lot of money, and skipped town.'

'How'd you come across this?' Barbara asked, her brow furrowing.

'A man named Duke got himself shot outside The

Garden of Eden. Madam Ophelia came into possession of a newspaper clipping that Duke was carrying on him. It was about Morley. Before he died, Duke told Madam Ophelia that he had seen Morley that day, here in Rio Diablo. Apparently, he had been tracking Morley for four years. We can assume that Morley saw him too, so the fellow ended up dead.'

'And you think Morley and Bonner are the same person?'

'Yep. Bonner showed up in Rio Diablo just about the time that Morley disappeared from Chicago with all that money.'

'But that could be coincidence,' Barbara mused. 'The fellow that Duke saw could be anyone. We've picked up a lot of people in the past five years, and not all of them are what you would call solid citizens.'

'That's true enough,' Stone admitted. 'I sure would like to talk to the police in Chicago about Richard Morley.'

'Why not telegraph them and ask? Say that you are a lawman.'

Stone smiled. 'I thought about that, but I think I'm being cold-trailed. If I sent a telegraph from here, Bonner's men or someone in the sheriff's department would know what was in it in about five minutes.'

'You'd have to go to Denton to send it,' Barbara said. 'That's a thirty-mile ride.'

'That's true,' Stone answered, 'but it may be worth it.'

Stone thought for a moment. 'I think I know how I can get out of town without Chalmers or Bonner knowing about it. You have a couple of good horses, don't you?'

'Yes, I do. And they are as good as any you'll find in the county.'

'I'll leave tonight. I'll come by after dark and put my horse in your barn. At midnight, when my shadow is convinced I'm spending another night here, I'll take one of your mounts and head for Denton. By sunup, I'll be half-way there. You'll go on to the shop like usual, and if anyone asks about me, you can be coy and just hint that I'm staying at your place now.'

Barbara threw back her head and laughed. 'Well, there goes what's left of my reputation!'

'Sorry about that,' Stone said. 'But I think you can manage.'

'Darned right!' Barbara chuckled. 'I'm rich enough that gossip just rolls off my back.'

At noon, Stone went into Mom's for lunch. While he was eating, Mom took a break from the kitchen and sat down at Stone's table.

'I don't know what you been doing, mister, but you sure as hell have some folks nervous 'round here,' she said, with a twinkle in her eye.

'What folks are you talking about?' he asked.

'Well, to begin with, C.J. Chalmer's people have been around asking about you. The first time any of 'em ever saw you, it was that day that you bounced old Luther Boggs out of here. For that reason, they seem to think the two of us are more than friends.' Mom winked suggestively and nudged Stone with her elbow, cackling. 'One of Chalmer's deputies came by here askin' 'bout you. Since I don't know nuthin', I couldn't tell him a thang. And when that deputy left, I watched him out the window, and he went down about half a block and had a long talk with that Smith what works for Boss Bonner. Or maybe it were Jones. Hell, I dunno which is which. Both of those odd birds look alike to me.'

'Thanks for the information, Mom. Yeah, I think they may be a little nervous. An honest lawman around here is something rare, I understand. And Mom, all I want to do is get even. Someone killed my partner, and I want to make it right.'

Another customer walked in and Mom got up. 'Just watch yer back, mister. We's had some mysterious back-shootin's round here.'

Stone smiled and nodded his understanding.

That evening, Stone gathered up his belongings and checked out of the hotel.

'Leavin' town?' the desk-clerk asked.

'Nope,' Stone told him. 'Just renting a room in a private home. Little bit cheaper than staying here.'

'Oh, I understand,' the clerk said. 'Well, good luck.'

Stone rode unhurriedly down California Street. As he passed the Lone Star saloon, he saw Smith standing in front, leaning against a post. The two men exchanged nods, and Stone rode on at a steady pace to Barbara's house. He unsaddled his horse and got it settled in a stall with water and feed. He placed the saddle on the saddle-rack at the end of the barn by the door, and joined Barbara inside.

They ate a light supper in the kitchen, and as Stone was finishing, Barbara stood beside him and pressed her body to his arm and shoulder.

'That was a cold supper,' she said. 'The least I can do is give you a hot send-off.'

There were few preliminaries after they reached the bedroom, when clothes were discarded carelessly, the fire was stoked, covers were tossed aside and the two off them were in one another's arms.

At midnight, Stone reluctantly crawled out of Barbara's bed and dressed in the dark. Before putting on his hat, he leaned over the beautiful girl snuggled beneath the covers and kissed her forehead.

'I'll take the bay gelding,' he said.

'Be careful,' she whispered. 'I want you back here real soon.'

In the barn, Stone saddled the bay with one of the spare

saddles, leaving his own saddle to satisfy a curious eye. By dawn, he was well into Denton County.

Stone stopped once on the trip, long enough to water and rest his mount. He reached Denton in the late afternoon, and headed for the depot. At the telegrapher's office, he sat down and composed his message. It read:

Chief of Police, Chicago, Illinois.
Seeking information on fugitive Richard Morley, wanted in your jurisdiction for embezzlement. Suspect may be in this area. Reply to B. Stone, Denton, Texas.

The telegraph-clerk read over the message, lifted his eyebrows, then counted the words. Stone paid him, then said, 'I'll check back with you in the morning. In the meantime, if anyone asks you about the telegraph I sent, show them this.'

Stone handed the clerk a second form, on which he had written a message to the sheriff of Harris County asking about back pay. Along with the form, Stone gave the clerk a silver dollar.

'This is to make sure that no one sees the real message. Understand?'

The clerk smiled broadly. 'You betcha, Mr Stone. I go off duty at seven, so I'll keep the real one with me. I'll be back at eight in the morning.'

Stone found a stable and put up the bay for the night.

'Feed him well,' Stone told the stablekeeper. 'He's worked for it today.'

Stone went to a nearby hotel and signed in as Randall Miller.

It was noon the next day when the clerk went to his window and signaled Stone, who was sitting in the depot waiting-room. The reply read:

94

Richard Morley, fugitive since 25 September 1880. Wanted in connection with disappearance of $100,000 in investors' funds and for questioning in murder of Elizabeth Duke. Description: five feet, ten inches; weight approx. 185 pounds; now fifty years old, dark hair, brown eyes. Four-inch knife wound scar on right forearm. Advise immediately if identification made. Use caution. Morley arrested at age sixteen for murder of adoptive parents. Insufficient evidence to indict.

G. Donohue, Chief.

'Get what you wanted?' the clerk asked, his eyes wide.

'Sure did, sonny,' Stone answered. 'Thanks for your help.'

'Hope you get 'im,' the clerk called, as Stone left the depot.

Stone didn't push the bay as he had when heading to Denton. Two hours after nightfall, he found a farmhouse where he and the gelding spent the night for seventy-five cents, breakfast included. From there, he rode on in to Rio Diablo, stopping once for the horse to rest and water.

Stone reached Rio Diablo at midday. Riding into town on the Denton road put him close to Silver City, so he made his first stop at The Garden of Eden. Ophelia and Shadrach hastily joined him in the parlor. He handed the Chicago police chief's message to Ophelia, and she read it aloud.

'So Mr Duke was looking for his daughter's killer,' Ophelia said grimly, when she finished reading. 'The poor man. Well, at least I hope he's found her.'

Stone smiled. 'Ophelia, you mean to tell me that you believe in heaven?'

'Nothing wrong with hedging your bets, Stone,' Ophelia replied.

Stone chuckled. 'The important thing is that the description the chief gives fits our Mr Bonner like a glove. To confirm that he's Morley, we need for someone to get a look at that right forearm.'

'Fat chance,' Ophelia snorted. 'You never see him without long sleeves. Even in the hottest weather, he doesn't roll them up. If he's Morley, now we know why.'

'There might be an easier way,' Shadrach said.

'How's that?' Stone wondered.

'There's a black man what works for Mr Bonner, named Jeffrey. Does all kinds of odd jobs for the gentleman. Works as a kind of butler at times, irons clothes, washes shirts, cleans up, that kind of thing. I know him pretty well, and I might be able to find out from him about that knife scar.'

'You'll have to be damned careful, Shadrach. Don't let on what we know,' Ophelia cautioned.

'Don't you worry, Miss Ophelia. I have a plan.'

Stone rose to go. 'Ophelia, put that telegraph message in your safe, along with the newspaper clipping. I suspect we are going to need some proof when this thing comes to a head.'

'How are we going to deal with Bonner, his men *and* C.J. Chalmers, Stone?' Ophelia asked, with concern.

'We're going to get some help, Ophelia. If Shadrach can verify the scar on Bonner's arm, we'll send messages to the chief of police in Chicago and the Texas Rangers. Maybe this thing can be cleared up without getting anyone shot.'

Stone turned toward the door. 'In the meantime,' he continued, 'I have a borrowed horse I've got to return.'

'Wouldn't have borrowed it from a certain young lady, would you?' Ophelia enquired, with a sly smile.

'Might have,' Stone said, straight-faced.

As Stone rode out of Silver City, he met Mush Bourland

on his buckboard heading toward The Eroticia, and rode directly in front of him, forcing him to rein his rig to a stop.

'Mr Bourland,' Stone said cheerily. 'We never did finish talking about our mutual friend.'

'Mutual friend? Who's that?'

Stone tilted his hat back on his head. 'The one that's stinking up a grave over in Fort Worth's Potter's Field. Remember?'

Bourland paled visibly. 'Don't know what you're talking about, Stone. Let me by.'

With that, Bourland whipped his horse and rolled on, the sweat clearly visible on his face.

Stone smiled to himself and rode on up California Street. He didn't have time for Bourland. He was looking forward to a hot bath, a home-cooked supper, and a famil-iar, friendly bed.

CHAPTER 10

When Stone awoke the next morning, while it was still dark, he lay there listening to Barbara's slow, steady breathing and enjoying the warmth of her body next to his. He thought he could hear voices from the rear of the house, one of which sounded like Bessie.

He turned on his side and put his arm around Barbara's body, marveling at the heat of it. When she responded by pressing her back against him, he started to feel the old, familiar stirring. He kissed her neck, and she took his hand and placed it over her left breast, pushing down gently on it. Suddenly the bedroom door burst open, and a bull's-eye lantern shone directly on them, blinding Stone.

'Hold it right there, Stone!' a gruff voice cried. Then there were hands pulling him out of the bed into the chill of the room. Seeing only the silhouette of a man in front of him, he lashed out with a straight right to the shadow's jaw, and was rewarded by the satisfying crack of his knuckles on a chin. The owner of the chin crumpled to the floor, toppling a small table.

Stone heard the click of a six-shooter hammer being cocked, and the same rasping voice cried, 'I'll kill you where you stand if you try that again.'

Someone lit a lamp from the bedside table, and Stone

recognized Sheriff Chalmers holding a gun on him. The deputy that Stone had floored was trying, somewhat unsteadily, to regain his feet.

'You all right, Terry?' Chalmers asked of the deputy.

'What in hell is this about, Chalmers?' Stone shouted.

'Yes, what in hell *is* this about?' Barbara cried from the bed. 'Do you have a warrant to be in my house?'

Chalmers looked at Barbara, who was holding the bedcovers up to her chin, and smiled. 'Yes, Miss, I certainly do,' he answered, holding up the document.

'On what grounds?' Barbara demanded.

'On the grounds that you are harboring a murderer,' Chalmers answered smugly. He turned to Stone and announced, 'Brimmer Stone, you are under arrest for the murder of Beauregard Worthington Bourland, otherwise known as Mush.'

'*What?*' Stone blurted. 'What in hell are you talking about?'

'Well, Mr Stone,' Chalmers oozed, almost joyfully, 'it seems that you showed up at The Eroticia last night about midnight demanding to see Mr Bourland. You forced your way into his office, and a few minutes late Big Sally goes to check and she finds him behind his desk with his throat cut from ear to ear. Hell of a mess!'

'That's bullshit and you know it, Chalmers,' Stone growled.

'Yes, it's bullshit!' Barbara cried. 'At midnight, he was right here with me.'

Chalmers smiled evilly at Barbara. 'Well, we'll see about that, won't we, Missy?'

While two deputies stood on either side of Stone, Luther Boggs, the sheriff's dim nephew, had edged his way to the other side of the bed. 'He's nekkid,' Luther grinned. 'Let's see what *she's* got on.' He started to pull back the bedclothes that covered Barbara.

Barbara reached out with her right hand and clawed at Luther's eyes. Streaks of blood erupted from the deputy's face.

'Oh, Gawdamighty!' Luther cried. 'She clawed my eyes out!'

Chalmers looked exasperated. 'Luther, you dumb shit! Get the hell away from that woman!'

Sobbing, Luther staggered away from the bed. Chalmers stopped him and looked at his face. 'She missed your eyes, dummy. You can quit your whimpering.' He shook his head, muttering, 'Jesus! My sister's only child.'

He turned back to Stone. 'Get your clothes on, Stone. You're goin' with us.'

Chalmers picked up the clothes that Stone had thrown hastily over the back of a chair, patted them down and found the billy. He put it in his pocket and handed the clothes to Stone. Stone looked at the two deputies holding their weapons on him, and got into his clothes, taking his time. After he dressed, Chalmers pulled his arms behind him and clamped manacles on his wrists.

As two deputies escorted him out the door, Stone looked at Barbara over his shoulder and said, 'Let 'em know.'

Barbara nodded her understanding.

Chalmers stopped in the door, turned, and tipped his hat to Barbara.

'Sorry for the inconvenience, Miss,' he grinned, and walked out, trailed by a chastened Luther.

They passed a distraught Bessie in the kitchen. 'I'm sorry, Mr Stone,' she sobbed. 'They said if I cried out, they'd kill me.'

'It's all right, Bessie, don't worry about it,' Stone answered. 'Just see to Miss Carrington.'

Outside, Terry Marion, the deputy who had taken the fist to his chin, let go of the arm he was holding and swung his right fist into Stone's stomach. Stone, unprepared, doubled over.

'Now, Terry,' Chalmers said, soothingly, 'that's enough of that. Be patient.'

Stone grimaced and straightened up, trying to catch his breath.

'You're a tough son of a bitch when someone's got their hands manacled behind them, aren't you, Terry?' he said, from between clenched teeth.

'I'll show you how tough,' Terry blurted. With his face reddening, he stepped in front of Stone and drew brass knuckles from his hip pocket.

'Terry!' the sheriff shouted, grabbing the deputy's arm. 'God damn it, cool down! I don't want any marks on that man.'

Marion stopped, staring at Stone. He then slowly returned the weapon to his pocket. Leaning forward till his nose almost touched Stone's, he said, 'Just wait, you son of a bitch, your turn is acomin'.'

'Try your best shot, Nancy-boy,' Stone sneered.

Marion screamed in rage and seized Stone by the throat. Stone reacted by throwing his right knee up into the deputy's crotch, almost lifting him off the ground. With a loud grunting explosion of air from his lungs, the deputy fell backward on to the ground, clutching his abdomen.

Chalmers leaned over the suffering deputy and raged, 'Damned if this man isn't goin' to make capons out of the bunch of you 'fore he's through! Now, you dimwits do what I tell you and get this man down to the gaol before I have you all committed to the lunatic asylum for being so damned stupid!'

Stone was lifted on to the back of Chalmer's buckboard and endured a bumpy ride to the gaol while the third deputy, a hard-eyed man named Malone, sat beside the sheriff holding a six-shooter. Luther and Terry Marion rode alongside, on their own horses.

The gaol was what Stone expected: small, dirty and dark. The office stank of tobacco and burned coffee. The three cells were redolent with sweat and a faint odor of urine. A cot made of bare planks with a thin straw mattress was fixed to the wall in each cell. The mattress ticking was heavily soiled and stained with various body fluids. Dim light was supplied by a lantern on the wall, out of reach of the cells.

Malone pushed Stone into the middle cell and removed the manacles while the sheriff covered him with his six-gun. Slamming the cell door shut with a clang, Malone said, 'If you have to take a shit, call out and some-body'll take you out in back to the privy. If you have to take a leak, use the bucket under the bed.'

'Thanks, I'll try to remember that,' Stone said, without emotion.

Stone examined the cot's mattress as well as he could under the dim light, and shoved it to the floor. He sat on the bare planks and pondered his situation. Then he became aware of someone in the cell to his right. He got up and peered through the bars at a figure lying on the cot.

'You asleep, neighbor?' Stone asked.

'Not hardly,' was the answer. 'With all the noise your friends made bringin' you in, how's a body 'sposed to get any sleep?' The man rose and put his hand through the bars. 'Bennie Lee Chandler,' he said.

Stone took the offered hand and shook it, introducing himself.

'Brimmer Stone?' Chandler repeated. 'Don't tell me your friends call you "Brim".'

'That's what they call me,' Stone answered.

Chandler threw back his head and laughed a long,

wheezing laugh. 'Brimstone! By God, that's good.' He cocked an eye at Stone and asked, 'Bring any hellfire with you?'

Stone smiled. 'I reckon when I get out of this place, you may see some.'

Chandler chuckled. 'I'd like that,' he said, wiping at his nose.

Chandler was a smallish man of around fifty years, with a two-day growth of beard and, as Stone's nose told him, he was not too clean. 'What you in for?' he asked.

'Murder. They claim I cut a man's throat,' Stone answered.

'Whooey!' Chandler exclaimed. 'Whose throat?'

'Mush Bourland.'

'Do tell! Old Mush is singing with the choir invisible, eh?'

'Somehow I doubt he's doing anything heavenly,' Stone chuckled.

'Did ya do it?'

'Nope. That's the excuse for getting me off the streets. I was finding out too much.'

Chandler reacted with surprise. 'Damnation, fellow! Ya sure 'nuf know how to get in trouble in Rio Diablo, don't ya? Big surprise is yer still alive.' Again, the wheezy laugh.

Stone asked, 'What did they get you for?'

'The usual, drunk and disorderly,' Chandler answered.

'You a frequent guest here?'

' 'Bout every other week; whenever I can get together the price of a bottle. I get a little loud at times, and most of the time I let my alligator mouth overload my kildee ass. I buggered the pooch this time, though. Broke out a couple of winders. Got to go 'fore the judge on Friday.' He yawned expansively. 'I sure enjoy jawin' with you, Brimstone, but I gotta get some sleep.'

'Go on, Bennie Lee, get some sleep,' Stone said. 'See

you in the morning.'

Chandler stretched out on his bunk and immediately began snoring.

Stone sat on his bunk, listening to the movements and activity in the office until dawn.

Malone had pulled the all-night duty, and he woke at six o'clock, went out the back to relieve himself, and came back in to make coffee on the office's wood-burning stove. Soon, the aroma of brewing coffee filled the cell area, and Bennie Lee stirred.

'Hey, out thar!' he called. 'How 'bout some of that coffee?' He looked at Stone and winked.

'Hold your horses, Bennie Lee,' Malone answered from the office. 'I'm cookin' it fast as I can.'

Shortly, Malone kicked open the door to the cells and entered carrying two tin cups. He handed them through the bars to his two prisoners.

'I'm givin' you two coffee 'fore I have any myself, 'cause you didn't raise no hell last night and let me sleep. I 'preciate that.'

The two prisoners drank their coffee in silence until they heard Malone exclaim, 'Who the hell's that?'

They heard the front door open and Madam Ophelia, in her best commanding voice, declared, 'Deputy, I understand you have a prisoner here named Stone. I've brought him some breakfast.'

Malone was confused. 'Well, ma'am,' he said, 'I usually go over to the bakery and get a left-over loaf of bread and give it to the prisoners for their breakfast.'

'Bread and water?' Ophelia cried. 'This isn't the dark ages, Deputy. Step aside and let me give my friend a decent meal.'

'Well, all right,' Malone said. 'But I'll have to check it for files and firearms and such.'

'Well, get on with it!' Ophelia ordered.

In a moment, Madam Ophelia and Aunt Josie, her cook, were bustling through the door. Aunt Josie carried a large tray, covered by a white linen cloth. The aroma of bacon filled the cells.

Aunt Josie put down the tray on a rough table against the wall, and pulled off the linen to reveal a bowl of scrambled eggs, a plate heaped high with bacon and sausages, a plate of biscuits and a bowl of cream gravy. Stone suddenly realized that he was hungry.

'Miss Ophelia, you and Aunt Josie are angels of mercy,' Stone said, as Ophelia handed him a shining white plate through the bars and began ladling out the food.

'I thought you might appreciate some decent food,' Ophelia boomed. Then her voice dropped to a whisper. 'Your Miss Carrington came this morning before dawn and got me up. When she told me what had happened, I was hoppin' mad. The two of us drank coffee for two hours, getting acquainted and making some plans.'

'You gonna eat all that yourself, Stone?'

Stone and Ophelia looked up to see Chandler watching them hungrily.

'How about giving some of this to Bennie Lee?' Stone suggested.

'Sure,' Ophelia said. 'Josie fixed enough for a posse.' She turned to the little man watching them. 'Bennie Lee, I should have known you'd be here. Need something to eat?'

'Yessum,' Bennie answered, eyeing the food.

Ophelia nodded to Josie, who handed Bennie a plate and heaped it with food. Bennie dug in happily. 'I like the crowd you run with, Stone,' he said between gulps. 'You oughta come here more often.'

'What are they up to, Stone?' Ophelia asked in a whisper. 'They can't make that kind of charge stick with Barbara Carrington standing up for you.'

105

Stone said in a loud voice, 'This sure is good chow, Aunt Josie.' Then whispering, he leaned close to Ophelia. 'I don't figure they even plan to take it to a grand jury. I figure they're going to try some way to shut me up before that happens. Or, even worse, do something to Barbara.'

'When do you think they'll try something?'

'Probably tonight. I'm going to need some help.'

Ophelia thought for a moment. 'I think I can manage that. By the way, Stone, Shadrach found out what we wanted to know.'

'The scar?'

'Yep, right where it was supposed to be. Shadrach got it out of the fellow that buttles for Bonner.'

'That cinches it,' Stone growled. 'We need to contact the Rangers and the chief of police in Chicago. Can you send a couple of telegraphs and sign my name to them?'

'I'll write them out and have one of the girls send them. They're watching me,' Ophelia whispered.

'Another thing,' Stone added. 'Get Barbara to stay out at your place tonight. She's a sitting duck over at that house of hers.'

'Will do,' the madam assured him. 'Watch your back.'

With a great bustle, Ophelia and Aunt Josie gathered up the dishes and silverware and walked back through the office to their carriage, where Shadrach waited. Bennie Lee lay on his cot, a smile of satisfaction on his face. He had polished off what Stone hadn't eaten, and he patted his stomach contentedly.

Madam Ophelia had just left when Stone heard another familiar voice in the office. In a few moments, the door opened and Terry Marion swaggered in. He looked at the two prisoners and smiled.

'The town drunk and the outlaw lawman. You two make quite a pair,' he said. 'But we'll be shut a'both of you pretty soon. Good riddance to bad trash.'

'What do ya mean by that?' Bennie Lee asked, his voice barely above a squeak.

'He's blowing smoke up your ass, Bennie Lee,' Stone growled. 'Don't worry about him. He won't do anything to you unless you're manacled.'

Marion roared a stream of curses. 'You just wait, Mr High and Damn Mighty, Mr Fast Draw,' he spat. 'We'll see who has the last laugh.'

Bennie was chuckling loudly.

'Shut up, you little sack of shit!' Marion bellowed at him. 'Two wise-asses. Two *dead* wise-asses,' he sneered. With that, he turned on his heel and stalked out.

'I think you've done it now, Brimstone,' Bennie whispered.

'I hope I have, Bennie,' Stone responded. 'When the time comes, I want him so damned angry he's not thinking about doing his job, but about getting even with me.'

'I'd say you accomplished that,' Bennie said ruefully.

CHAPTER 11

Stone passed the day sitting on the planks of his cot and dozing from time to time. On occasion, he heard C.J. Chalmers in the office issuing orders to his deputies or relating a humorous story for the benefit of visitors.

Bennie Lee needed a drink and, with each passing hour, he became more restive, finally starting to pace his cell.

At one o'clock, Brim heard Barbara's voice in the office, mixing with Chalmer's wheedling tones. Finally, the door to the cells opened and Barbara walked in, accompanied by a tall, gray-haired man whom Stone did not recognize. Barbara introduced the man as Harold Curtis, an attorney. As the two men men shook hands through the bars, she explained that Curtis was the attorney for the cotton gin and that she had gone to him for advice. She said that she had approached Rio Diablo's three attorneys about defending Stone, and had been politely but firmly turned down.

Curtis spoke softly, so as not to be overheard in the outer office. 'The attorneys here in Rio Diablo are afraid to touch you, Stone. The word is out from Bonner's camp that they are not to bother.'

Stone's lips curled into a crooked smile. 'Why am I not

surprised at that news?' he drawled. 'I kept putting the pressure on Mush Bourland, and he wasn't taking it well. The problem is that I underestimated Bonner's ruthlessness. He got rid of a potential leak and me at the same time.'

'So Barbara told me,' Curtis said. 'I'll represent you through the preliminary hearing, and I'll try to get you out of this place on bond. But I'm a corporate attorney, not a criminal lawyer. As far as the trial goes, we'll need someone with heavy experience in criminal law, like Hayter over in Denton County.'

'I've got a feeling that it won't come to that,' Stone said. 'I think they'll try to resolve the whole thing before it gets to a jury.'

Barbara was wide-eyed. 'Do you . . .' she blurted but Stone quickly held his trigger finger to his lips. She tried again, this time in a whisper. 'Do you think they'll try to . . . I mean . . . something to you?'

Stone nodded. 'Deputy Marion made a little slip this morning, which sort of confirmed what I had been thinking. They can't get away with it unless they get you out of the way or I don't live long enough to go to trial.'

Barbara's face paled. 'What are you going to do?' she whispered.

'Help is on the way,' Stone answered. 'Shadrach is my way out of here.'

Curtis looked grim. 'I hope so, Stone,' he said. 'Miss Carrington,' he whispered, 'we have to act as if we know nothing about this.' Then, in a loud voice, he added, 'Mr Stone, we'll arrange to post bond. Perhaps I can have you out of here by tomorrow.'

'And I'll bring you some supper tonight,' Barbara said. 'How about that beef stew that you like?'

'Sounds good,' Stone replied, with a smile. 'I'll see you this evening.'

*

That evening, when Barbara put in her appearance, carrying a tray covered with a white cloth, Luther had just taken Bennie Lee out the back to the privy and was locking his cell. Anticipating her entry into the cell area, Luther left the office door open, giving Stone a direct view into the office. The unkempt Terry Marion was sitting behind the sheriff's desk.

'Hold it a minute there, Missy,' Marion said. 'What you got there?'

Barbara stopped and said in a business-like tone, 'I have some beef stew, cornbread and chocolate pie for Mr Stone's supper.' She looked directly at Stone in his cell, and smiled.

'Whooey!' Marion exclaimed. 'The prisoners are gettin' better fed than the deputies. Well, I have to take a look under that cloth.'

'Go ahead, but hurry up. I don't want it to get cold,' Barbara said impatiently.

Marion arose languidly from behind the desk, scratching at his rear end, and sauntered to where Barbara stood. He looked at Barbara's lips and made a kissing motion with his own. Disgust rose in Barbara's eyes.

Marion lifted the white cloth covering the tray and inspected the food carefully. Then he said, 'Got to make sure you ain't hiding no knives or nothing in that stew.' He reached into the bowl of stew with his bare and obviously filthy right hand, and stirred it around. Barbara's eyes flashed her outrage. 'Damn, sure is hot!' Marion exclaimed, grinning and wiping his hand with the white cloth. 'But there ain't no weapons in there.' He turned to wink at Luther.

Barbara said nothing, but when Marion turned back to her, she upended the tray in his face. He howled and staggered back, beef stew and hot coffee covering his face and shoulders. Whipped cream from the pie was slathered along the left side of his head.

Luther roared with laughter.

As Marion struggled to clear his eyes, Barbara turned on her heel and marched out the door.

Marion exploded into a torrent of invective so blasphemous and filthy that even Luther stopped laughing to listen in amazement.

Stone stood against the bars of his cell, grinning at Barbara's reaction and Marion's rage. When Marion finally got his eyes clear enough to see Stone's grin, he flew into a new rage.

'Laugh now, you son of a bitch,' he shouted at Stone, stew dripping from his hair. 'We're gonna fix you and that bitch-whore of yours.'

At that moment, Chalmers walked through the front door and roared, 'Shut that damned mouth!' He stopped and stared at Marion. 'What in the hell happened to *you?*'

Marion was speechless, but Luther broke in. 'He stuck his hand in Miss Carrington's stew and she dumped it on him,' he said, chuckling.

Chalmers moved to the door leading to the cells and slammed it shut. 'If I make it through this day's business, it'll be a damned wonder!' he exclaimed. 'You, you stupid fool,' he spat, thrusting his face into Marion's, 'do you run off at the mouth about every damned thing you know? And why did you outrage that Carrington woman? If Bonner hears about this, my ass won't hold shucks.'

Stone listened to Chalmer's tirade through the closed door. After he heard Chalmers order Marion to go home and change clothes 'before Bonner gets here', he settled back on his cot to wait.

Just before ten o'clock, the door opened and C.J. Chalmers walked in. He avoided Stone's eyes and walked to Bennie Lee's cell. Unlocking the cell door, he said, 'Get on out of here, Bennie Lee. We're turning you loose so you can go home.'

'I thought I had to wait here until the judge came on Friday,' Bennie squeaked in surprise.

'Hell, we know you ain't goin' to go nowhere,' Chalmers said. 'Just be back on Friday morning.'

Bennie was euphoric, and thanked the sheriff profusely as he exited the cell. But when he turned to say goodbye to Stone, a flicker of uncertainty crossed his face. 'You goin' to be all right, Brimstone?' he asked.

Stone smiled at his concern. 'Thanks, Bennie. Yeah, I'll be fine. Now get yourself on home. And stay out of trouble.'

A half-hour later, the door opened and Bonner himself walked in. He walked up to the bars and peered through at Stone, who was sitting on his bunk.

'Well, Stone, too bad it ends up like this. You could have had a good run if you'd taken me up on that job offer. Yes, indeed.' He leaned closer to the bars, sneering. 'But your personal integrity got in the way, didn't it, Stone? What do you call that, the Code of the West?' He laughed sarcastically. 'Your mistake was striking up that strange friendship of yours with that whoremaster.'

Stone showed no emotion while Bonner waited for a reply.

'You have anything to say?' Bonner asked, puzzled. 'This is your last chance to say anything, boy. Yes, indeed.'

Stone turned and looked at Bonner for the first time since the man had entered.

'Just remember, whatever happens from now on is on your shoulders, Bonner. And there is no backing out or quitting,' he said.

Bonner looked shocked but recovered and snorted, 'Big talk from a dead man,' then walked out.

Stone listened as Bonner spoke to the men standing in the office. 'Old C.J. and I are going down to the Lone Star for a drink. Wait about five minutes, and then do it.'

Then Chalmers said, 'You two get on out of here and see about that woman. Make it look good!'

Stone heard the front door close and a low murmur of voices from the office. He sat on his bunk, legs drawn up, head down on his knees as if he were sleeping. After a few minutes he heard the office door swing open, and the sound of tiptoeing feet on the stone floor. He heard the key turn in the rusty lock of his cell door, then a sudden rush of steps.

Stone raised his head and kicked with both feet into the stomachs of the two closest bodies. There were two satisfying grunts, and the pair fell backward into the two behind them. Then Stone was on his feet and swinging his fist into the face of the nearest man, Smith, who staggered back into the cell bars. Stone could see his assailants by the light of a lantern held by a wide-eyed deputy standing in the door. An evil-looking bearded thug was coming at him with three feet of rope in his hands.

The man tried to grab Stone around the neck, but Stone swung an elbow into his chest and followed up with a left hook. The two men on the floor were grasping at Stone's legs. Stone pulled one leg free and stamped down on a wrist. There was a cry of pain, but the other assailant grabbed Stone's legs in a bear hug. As he tried to extricate his legs, he was jumped from behind. As Stone swung at the beard, a bloody-faced Smith attacked him from the other side. With the man on the floor holding his legs together, Stone lost his balance and fell. Suddenly, heavy strong bodies were on top of him.

Just then, he heard the bearded man say, 'Hold him just like that so I can get this rope around his neck.'

It flashed through Stone's mind that he might have

come to the end of his all-too-short life, and he tried futilely to free his arm but the three men holding him knew their business. He felt a coarse rope slide around his neck.

Just then there was a thud somewhere outside the cell, and Stone heard a crash as the kerosene lantern broke. The deputy holding the lantern had fallen heavily to the floor. Stone heard the bearded guy cry: 'Shit! Fire!' There was another thud, and suddenly one of the weights atop him was removed. With one arm freed, Stone grasped the nearest face, digging his fingers into its eyes. The man fell backward, screaming. Stone turned and saw a goggle-eyed Smith looking with horror at something out of Stone's line of sight. There was a sickening splat as Shadrach's truncheon tore into Smith's face, and Smith tumbled backward, unconscious, his face a red pulp.

The fourth man tried to run, but Stone grabbed him by the ankles and pulled him to the floor. He rolled the man over and smashed his nose with a straight right to the face. The man screamed, covering his face with his hands, and blubbered, 'Don' hit me no more! Don' hit me no more"

Stone jumped to his feet, and he and Shadrach grabbed the unconscious deputy's arms and pulled him into the cell. Stone retrieved his hat from the cell and slammed the door shut. Shadrach picked up a key-ring from the floor where the deputy had dropped it, and locked the five men inside.

'Thanks, my friend,' Stone said to Shadrach. 'I owe you my life.'

'I'm glad I was on time. I cut it a little close,' Shadrach replied, wearing a broad grin.

'I think they've sent two men after Barbara,' Stone said, ripping open the sheriff's locked desk drawer and pulling out his billy and his .45. He flipped open the gun's cylinder to make certain it was still loaded. 'Is she out at the palace?'

Shadrach looked distressed. 'No, sir, not when I left. She said she had to get some things from home. But she told Miss Ophelia to leave the Garden and try to get out to the cotton gin without anyone seeing her. I think that's where Miss Carrington was going.'

Stone asked, 'Do you have your pistol?'

'Yessir. Two of 'em. And a double barrel twelve gauge in my saddle holster.'

'Then let's go,' Stone commanded.

Stone leaped astride one of the horses tied up in front of the gaol, while Shadrach ran across the street and behind a building. After a few moments, he emerged on his horse. The two spurred their mounts furiously toward the Carrington house.

For the first time, Stone had to fight back panic in the pit of his stomach. He had faced danger many times, but this was the first time someone he cared for was in mortal danger, and he realized she could already be dead. He told himself, 'You're no good if you lose control. Keep your wits. Do your job.'

As Stone and Shadrach galloped up to the Carrington house, they could see there were no horses out front. Stone continued his gallop to the back of the house. When he saw two horses tied up, his stomach turned over. He recognized Luther's and Marion's horses, the ones that had trotted alongside him during his buckboard trip to the gaol.

Stone leaped from the saddle and, drawing his weapon, raced to the back door, followed by Shadrach. A body wearing skirts was sprawled on the kitchen floor. Stone bent over it and saw that it was Bessie. There was no blood, but her head lay at an odd angle, her eyes open in the dim light.

Stone could hear the sounds of scuffling and furniture being upset from the front of the house. He strode into the hallway and almost stumbled over another body. It was Luther Boggs. He was lying on his back, with a faint look of surprise on his face. A neat hole had been punched in the center of his forehead, and a small rivulet of blood was trickling down from the hole into his hair. Stone noted there was no blood under Luther's head, which indicated that a low-velocity slug had dug a hole in Luther's thick skull but had not exited.

The sounds were coming from Barbara's bedroom. Stone threw open the door to see a disheveled Barbara struggling with Marion. Her blouse was torn half off, exposing her left breast. There was blood on her face. When Stone marched in, Marion swung Barbara around between the door and his own body, drawing his sidearm. He put the cocked .44 to the base of her skull.

'Drop it, Stone!' he ordered. 'Or I blow her damned head clean off.'

'Don't you do it, Brim,' Barbara yelled.

Marion grinned. 'You interrupted the party. I was just about to get me some of your bitch-whore.'

Stone's mouth curled sarcastically. 'With what, Nancy-boy?' he asked.

Marion's eyes widened and he roared in rage. His gun hand lashed out to fire at Stone. When Barbara felt the muzzle of his pistol leave her neck, she spun to her left. Stone fired from the waist and his shot struck Marion in the right side of his chest, knocking him backward against the wall. He got off one shot, but it hit the floor. When Marion tried to raise his pistol, Stone fired again. This time the slug hit Marion dead center in the breastbone, and smashed out through his back, spraying blood on Barbara's bedroom wallpaper. The dying man slid down the wall and slumped forward on his face.

116

CHAPTER 12

Stone took three strides, kicked the pistol away from Terry Marion's limp hand and leaned over to feel the deputy's neck for a pulse. Detecting none, he turned to Barbara. Taking her by the shoulders, he peered into her face.

'Are you all right? Did he hurt you?' he asked anxiously.

She put her arms around him, and he could feel her trembling. One sob of relief escaped her throat. Gathering strength from his embrace, she smiled gamely and said, 'Other than a split lip, a bloody nose and some wounded dignity, no.'

Stone breathed a sigh of relief.

Suddenly aware of her exposed breast, Barbara began tugging at her torn blouse to cover herself. 'What happened at the gaol?' she asked shakily.

'They'd planned a little necktie party,' Stone told her. 'They were going to strangle me with a rope, then hang me from the bars or some such to make it look like a suicide. But Shadrach came along with a limb off a piss-elm tree and changed their plans.'

'Then Luther and Terry Marion had a little more in mind for me than rape,' Barbara stated, matter-of-factly.

'That's right. With the suspect a suicide and the star witness a victim of burglars, they had nothing to worry about. It would have been a clean slate. By the way, I didn't

117

know you had a derringer.'

Barbara smiled ruefully. 'I don't tell everything I know, Stone. I started carrying it when this business started. Luther was rather surprised.'

'That was a nice shot, Miss Carrington,' Shadrach commented.

'Thanks,' she replied. 'I figured that shooting him in that big body of his wouldn't do a bit of good, so I aimed at his head. Judging from the way he went down, I must have been lucky and hit him in that pea brain of his. But while I was trying to cock the hammer for my second shot, Terry Marion knocked the gun out of my hand.' Suddenly her eyes widened. 'Bessie! What did they do to her?'

'I'm sorry about Bessie,' Stone answered softly. 'She's in the kitchen.'

With panic welling up in her face, Barbara rushed to the kitchen and bent over the body of her housekeeper.

'Bessie? Bessie?' she called, trying to rouse her. When no response came, she started weeping. 'Those bastards!' she cried, through her tears. 'They killed a decent gentlewoman for no other reason than that she happened to be here!'

Stone and Shadrach removed their hats and stood there while Barbara straightened Bessie's body and her clothes, and covered her with a clean sheet from the linen closet.

'If it's any comfort, Miss Carrington,' Shadrach offered, 'those two killers are standing before the highest judge right now.'

Barbara looked up. 'It will be a comfort to me when the rest of those vile people are with them.'

Suddenly, a figure appeared in the back door. In a split second, Stone had drawn and was prepared to fire. A gray-haired man in his shirtsleeves threw up his hands and shouted, 'I'm not armed!'

118

'It's all right, Brim,' Barbara cried. 'It's Mr Campbell, my next-door neighbor.'

Stone returned his pistol to its holster.

Campbell noticed Bessie's body and, horrified, asked, 'What in heaven's name has happened here, Barbara? I heard shots. Is Bessie dead?'

'Yes, she's dead,' Barbara answered. 'She was killed by two of C.J. Chalmer's men, who came out here to kill me.'

Barbara introduced Campbell to Stone and Shadrach, then quickly filled him in on the accusation against Stone and what had happened at the gaol. She explained that more people would be coming when the first two didn't return, and that she and her friends had to leave. She asked him if he would send someone to town to ask the undertaker to come after Bessie's body, and said that she would take care of the cost.

'Yes, of course, my dear,' Campbell said. 'So Bonner and Chalmers have come to this, have they? I wondered how long it would take them to start openly murdering people; they've done everything else.'

'We won't tell you where we're going, Mr Campbell,' Barbara said. 'So if they ask you where we are, you can truthfully say you don't know.'

Campbell smiled. 'Thank you, my dear; a wise decision. You go on and do what you have to do. I'll see to Bessie.'

He stopped and turned as he went out the door. 'Good luck to you and your friends, Barbara. Shoot straight!'

'Thanks,' she said. 'We'll need the luck.'

Stone commented grimly, 'You're right, we will need the luck. The sowbelly is in the fire now. It's going to be a fight to the finish, whether we want it or not. It's my guess that when that deputy fails to show up at the Lone Star saloon to announce my suicide, Bonner and Chalmers are going to check the gaol and put together a posse of Bonner's people. What weapons do you have in the house?'

'Other than my father's lever-action carbine, nothing,' Barbara told him.

'That's OK. It will help,' Stone said. 'Get it, and all the ammunition you have for it.'

Stone found his horse in the stall where he had left it the previous night and he saddled Barbara's favorite mount. Shadrach moved the two dead deputies' horses and the horse that Stone had taken from the gaol into the shed and out of sight.

Barbara appeared, carrying the short-barreled rifle. It was a Winchester Model 1866 .44 rimfire, and she shoved it into the scabbard attached to her saddle. She had changed clothes and was wearing a dark-colored riding outfit with a split skirt so she could straddle a horse. The three mounted and, with Barbara in the lead, they galloped through the night to the east, avoiding the direct route into town.

Barbara's knowledge of the town's byways served them well in the darkness. All habitations had passed behind them when they came to a crossroads, and Barbara reined her mount left, toward the north.

'This road will take us up behind the cotton gin in about two miles,' she explained. 'If they should be watching the road in front, they won't see us come in behind the warehouse.'

Soon they could see the dark shadow of the cotton gin in the moonlight, and slowed their mounts to a trot. The big, open-sided warehouse stood two hundred yards from the road they were on. Barbara turned off the road into the field.

'We better walk from here,' she said, in a soft voice.

The three dismounted and, leading their horses, walked across the stubble of the pasture to the sheltering darkness of the warehouse.

Barbara led them around the north side of the warehouse to a small stable. 'This is where we keep the mules,' she explained. 'There's plenty of room for the horses.'

Stone stopped suddenly. 'There's somebody over there with a horse,' he said.

Peering into the darkness, Shadrach announced, 'It's Miss Ophelia. She made it!'

'Shadrach, is that you?' Ophelia asked, out of the darkness.

'Yes, Miss Ophelia.'

'Thank goodness!' Ophelia said. 'I could hear noises in the dark and thought it might be Bonner's men. I was getting ready to shoot this thing.' She held up a long-barreled .44.

'Damn! I'm glad you didn't, Ophelia,' Stone chuckled. 'You might have killed all of us, and our horses. Speaking of horses, let's get these animals in the stable and out of sight.'

While they bedded down the horses, Ophelia explained how she got away without being followed. 'They had a man posted on the front porch of The Eroticia, keeping an eye on me,' she said. 'I spotted him early in the evening from my bedroom window and he was still there at eleven o'clock. But, all of a sudden, someone rides up and hollers to him, and he jumps on his horse and the two ride away like the devil was after 'em. I figured that was a good time, so I left Rosemary in charge and went out the back, where Shadrach had left my rig. I drove away like it was a Sunday afternoon and I don't think anyone noticed. I hadn't been here five minutes when you showed up.'

'They must have sent for your shadow when they found that mess we left in the gaol,' Stone said. 'By the way, did you get those telegraph messages sent?'

'Sure did,' Ophelia said proudly. 'I sent Mary Ruth and Norma Joyce down there with them. They both enjoyed the intrigue and I don't think anyone paid any attention

121

to them. And by the way, I brought that newspaper clipping and telegraph message with me, just in case they decided to rifle through my safe.'

'Good thinking,' Stone remarked.

Barbara unlocked the rear door of the gin's main office, and the group filed in behind her. 'We can't risk a light. Just feel your way around,' Barbara said. 'There are some chairs in here.'

Stone took up a post at the front window, peering out at the main road. He leaned forward to get a better look and said, 'There are two riders coming. Somebody must have thought of this place and sent a couple of guns out to take a look. I had hoped we would have time to make some plans, but we've got to deal with these two first.'

The small band waited silently as the two riders approached. The men slowed their horses to a walk, then stopped by a hitching rail. They dismounted, tied up their mounts and conferred quietly, their heads close together. They then drew their pistols and walked in opposite directions.

Stone turned to the others and whispered, 'They're going to take a look around. If they see our horses in that stable, it's all over.' To Shadrach, he continued, 'Get outside, stay in the shadow and watch the one that went to the south. I'll watch the one that went to the north. If he finds our horses, I'll stop him. You'll have to take care of the other one.'

Stone removed his light gray hat and put it on a table, then eased open the office's back door. 'Barbara, you've got that carbine. If anyone other than me or Shadrach tries to get in, you know what to do.'

The two men slipped silently into the night, and Barbara closed and bolted the door behind them.

Stone turned left and moved silently along the building's outside wall, staying in the shadow of the eaves. He came to a rain barrel at the corner of the building, and crouched behind it, listening. He heard footsteps on the gravel and the gunman came into view. The man hesitated, then turned toward the stable. He listened for several seconds at the door then tried it. Finding it unlocked, he pulled the door open far enough to slide inside. Through the partially open door, Stone could see the flare of a match.

It didn't take long for the gunman to see the three saddled horses in the stalls, and he came rushing out through the open door.

'Hold it, and drop your gun!' Stone commanded.

The startled gunman spun and blindly fired at Stone's voice, and tried to get back through the stable door. Stone fired, and the gunman jerked and grunted as the slug struck him in the side. But the gunman had seen Stone's muzzle-flash, and he raised his pistol and fired, hitting the rain barrel. Stone fired again, and this time the gunman lurched backward to the ground, limbs thrashing. Within three seconds, Stone heard Shadrach's twelve-gauge speak from several yards away. Stone waited, but there was no answering shot. He walked to the fallen gunman and felt for a pulse. He felt the irregular pulse slow, then stop. He turned and headed in the direction of Shadrach's shot.

Stone found him bending over a motionless figure on the ground. The corpse lay on its back, the chest a bloody mess.

'When he heard the shots, he started running,' Shadrach said. 'I didn't want him to come up behind you.'

'Thanks, my friend, once again.' Stone smiled. 'Let's get these two out of sight and then see to their horses. When they don't report back to Bonner, they're going to send someone else out here. Let 'em come. In the meantime, we'll make our plans.'

Back in the office with Barbara and Ophelia, Brim said,

'We're going to have to fight so we won't fight on their turf; we'll make them fight on ours. The question is: how many men can they muster for a fight?'

'Can we have a light now, Brim?' Barbara asked.

'I think it'll be safe for right now,' Brim said.

Barbara lit a kerosene lantern while Ophelia closed the drapes across the front window, then produced a sheet of paper from a desk. She wrote 'Chalmers' and 'Bonner' at the top, separated by a vertical line.

Barbara looked at her companions and said, 'Chalmers has, or rather had, four deputies.' Then she wrote the names under the Chalmers heading, calling them out as she wrote: 'Marion, Boggs, Malone and Gibbs. Of course,' she added, marking through two names, 'we can scratch off Marion and Boggs.'

Stone chuckled. 'Gibbs must have been the one that Shadrach put down when he came into the gaol. Do you think he's walking, Shadrach?'

'I don't rightfully know,' Shadrach told him, scratching behind an ear. 'I got in a pretty good lick. He may or may not be back on his feet, depending on how thick his skull is.'

'Put a question mark by his name,' Stone said. 'That leaves one that we know is healthy: Malone. Now, how about Bonner's men?'

'There's Smith and Jones,' Ophelia offered.

'Smith will be lucky if he's walking around after that lick to the face that Shadrach gave him. But there were also the two that were helping Smith,' Stone said. 'Don't know their names, they didn't introduce, themselves.'

Barbara, writing, said, 'There's Jones and maybe Smith. I'll put a question mark beside his name. Then there are thugs One and Two. How many more gun hands does Bonner have?'

'At least two more,' Ophelia declared. 'It's my impression that he kept an even half-dozen. In fact, I heard one of my customers say something about "that half-dozen 'prison escapees' that Bonner keeps on his payroll".'

'Well, two of that half-dozen are fertilizing the weeds out back right now. So that leaves four men he can rely on. At least one of those is questionable,' Stone said. 'Of course, he can always find a couple of cowhands or loafers who will sign on to do some dirty work for a few dollars. They will draw fire while the regulars do the real work. Barbara, don't I see some sort of short bridge on the road, about fifty yards from here?'

'Yes,' Barbara replied. 'There's a bridge over a dry gully that cuts across the road. It has water in it when we have a heavy rain.'

Stone turned to Shadrach. 'With you in that gully under the bridge, and me up on the roof with the carbine, we'll have them in a crossfire. I should be able to get two of them, maybe three, before they can take cover or run. When they head back your way, you use that twelve-gauge.'

Shadrach nodded.

'Leave the lantern burning and the drapes open just a crack so that they can see a light, and you ladies take cover somewhere else. If they get past us, it'll be up to you to finish them off,' Stone said grimly.

Shadrach produced a pistol from under his jacket. 'Here, Miss Barbara. Hold on to this. It's a double action .38. It'll be more accurate than that derringer.'

'Thanks,' Barbara said, admiring the pistol. 'But how about you?'

Shadrach patted a shoulder holster. 'I've still got something in reserve.'

Barbara turned and gently kissed Stone on the lips. She handed him the carbine and the spare ammunition, and the two men slipped out the door into the night.

CHAPTER 13

Outside, Stone took Shadrach by the arm.

'If *I* were sending two men out to find if someone was hiding in a particular place, I'd tell them if they found anything, that one should stay and keep watch, and the other should ride back and let me know what they found. When neither of those two show up back in town, Bonner's people will probably be out in strength, so our best defense is to get them first. Let's hope they all ride past the bridge, so you'll be at their backs. If all of them don't, we'll have to deal with that as it happens. Are you ready?'

'I'm ready,' Shadrach answered. 'You'll be up on the roof?'

'Yes, and I'll wait till they are pretty close, so I'll be firing downward. That should keep you out of my line of fire. And I'll be far enough away from you that your scattergun won't get me.'

'Good luck,' Shadrach said, extending his hand.

Stone clasped the offered hand tightly. 'Thanks, and the same to you.'

The two men parted in the darkness, Shadrach to trot out to the bridge, and Stone to clamber up to the roof of the office building.

Stone had settled into position. From where he lay, just

126

behind the roof's peak, the roof sloped downward, giving him an unobstructed view of the road, bridge and ground in front of the office. He heard Barbara's voice from below.

'Stone,' she said in a stage whisper, 'Ophelia and I are going to hide in the tool shed at the corner of the warehouse. There's only one door, so if they try to get in, we'll have two guns on 'em.'

'Good idea. Take care of yourself. I've got plans for a big Saturday night.' He could hear Barbara's throaty chuckle as the two women made their way to the tool shed.

Stone had time to think about many things as he lay atop the roof. His comment to Barbara about Saturday night was just swagger. He knew that unless they were very fortunate, or their opponents were very stupid, he and that beautiful brown-eyed girl might not be alive when Saturday night came. This thing would continue until he, or Bonner, and several others were dead. He thought about Grady, and that it was his idea to come up here to Rio Diablo. He wondered if Grady were sitting somewhere watching all this and laughing at the joke.

After less than an hour, Stone learned that his earlier suppositions had been correct. He could hear the sound of galloping horses from the south. The night was in its last hour, and Stone could see the riders by the meager starlight. As they neared the bridge, Stone's stomach turned over as he counted six riders. They pulled to a halt just the other side of the bridge where Shadrach was hiding. They conferred, then started moving again. Stone could hear the hoofs drumming on the wooden bridge as they passed over it. After the group passed over the bridge, two riders broke off and rode in a westerly direction, paralleling the gully. Immediately, Stone knew they planned to circle around to the north end of the cotton gin and approach their quarry from behind.

The remaining four slowed to a trot as they approached the gin office. Before they had a chance to rein in their horses, Stone aimed carefully at the nearest rider, and fired. The slug struck the man solidly in the chest and he fell backward, dropping the reins. Before he fell from his saddle, Stone had levered another cartridge into the rifle's chamber and fired again. The second rider cried out in pain and turned his horse, spurring it frantically back the way he came. As he passed the other two riders, they hesitated for only a split second before they too abandoned their original plans and started riding for their lives.

Stone stood up and took aim at the wounded man rapidly receding into the darkness. When he fired, the galloping horse buckled and fell, catapulting the rider over the horse's head into the dirt of the road. Stone realized he had hit the horse instead of the rider.

The two remaining riders were intent on putting as much distance as possible between themselves and the unseen rifleman, and were looking back over their shoulders when Shadrach walked on to the road in front of them. Stone heard two shotgun blasts followed by thirty seconds of silence. Then there was a single report of a pistol shot. Straining his eyes, Stone finally made out the broad-shouldered figure of Shadrach trotting toward him. Stone skimmed down the roof and dropped from the eave on to the ground.

'Well?' Stone asked, peering into the darkness.

'There are two less riders working for Bonner,' Shadrach informed him. 'And that one who got his horse shot out from under him has a broken neck.'

'What was that pistol shot?'

'I hit one of the horses pretty bad, had to put it out of its torment. Where did the other two go?'

'Rode around to the north,' Stone said, reloading the carbine as he walked rapidly toward the shadows between

128

the buildings. 'They planned on coming up behind us while we dealt with the other four. The fact that the four didn't last long may have screwed up their plans. I'll bet good money that they are experienced guns that have been with Bonner for a while. The four dead ones were probably hired out of a saloon.'

'I won't call that bet. They acted like amateurs,' Shadrach agreed.

Stone stopped and peered around the corner of the office building. 'Sun-up can't be too far off,' he said, glancing at the eastern horizon. 'I don't think it will pay to try to find those two. Why don't we just sit tight and let them come to us?'

'Good thinking,' Shadrach said. 'I'll take the rain barrel.'

'Good,' Stone agreed. 'I'm going to camp over those crates by the warehouse corner. I'll be able to see you from there, and you can see me. That way, we can watch each other's backs.'

They took their places on either side of the narrow lane that ran between the office and warehouse down to the stable. Silence fell over the sprawling cotton gin as the eastern horizon started to lighten. After a few minutes, Shadrach motioned and pointed to the north then held up one finger. As Stone watched, Shadrach mouthed 'stable'. Stone nodded his understanding. He knew that if one of the gunmen was behind the stable, the other could be anywhere. He shifted his position slightly so he could see across the floor of the warehouse.

The warehouse was a large expanse of open storage, floored with heavy planks and roofed with corrugated sheet metal. Walls were unnecessary, since heat or cold did not affect the cotton bales stored there. A railroad spur serviced the loading dock on the warehouse's east side. The roof-supporting posts arranged at regular intervals across the warehouse floor were eight by eights and too narrow to conceal a man. With the rising sun, a breeze came up, disturbing and rattling sheets of the metal roof.

Stone hated the waiting, but the fact that the two gunmen had time to establish defensive positions made any attempt to ferret them out too risky. He hoped they would grow impatient and attempt to move on him and Shadrach. He knew the gunmen had no way of knowing how many people they were stalking, and that fact was probably making them cautious.

Suddenly, Stone heard a peculiar sound among the rattles of the warehouse's metal roof. He wasn't sure whether it was just another wind-blown rattle, or something different. Then he heard it again, the noise of a metal sheet being depressed and springing back into place. He stared at the rafters of the warehouse, trying to discern any trace of movement on the roof. Then, made visible by the rising sun behind it, a trace of dust and tiny pieces of debris wafted down from the rafters toward the warehouse floor. As he watched, there was another, almost imperceptible cascade of dust in the sun's rays. This time, it was closer to where he crouched and Stone became aware that gunman number two was on the roof. He thought about firing through the roof, but realized he would be firing blind and the probability of his shots being deflected by the wooden structure was too high.

He glanced at Shadrach. Shadrach, crouching behind the rain barrel at the corner of the office building, could not see up on the warehouse roof and was in a vulnerable position. The gunman could suddenly appear at the edge of the roof and have the drop on him. Stone waved his left arm. Shadrach saw the movement from the corner of his eye and looked at Stone. When Stone pointed to the roof, Shadrach glanced up and realized how vulnerable was his position.

Shadrach glanced down the alley toward the stable, then gathered himself and leaped from his hiding place, sprinting across the alley toward where Stone waited. There was a shot, and dust kicked up six feet behind Shadrach. The burly man hit the ground and rolled. Stone put down the carbine, drew his .45 and jumped from behind the crates. He ran to the south edge of the warehouse, turning so he could see the roof. Stone and the roof gunman saw one another simultaneously. The gunman fanned off two shots from the waist and Stone heard one of them buzz past his ear. He extended his arm and fired once. The gunman staggered back and fired wildly, the shot going into the air. Stone took careful aim and fired again. The gunman lurched backward, fell, and slid a few feet down the gently sloped roof, leaving a smear of blood.

Stone called to Shadrach, 'I'm going around the warehouse to get behind the other one.'

He trotted down the south side of the warehouse and up the east side by the railroad tracks, reloading as he went. Reaching the north-east corner, he stopped and, crouching down, peered cautiously around. The remaining gunman, unaware that he was now the sole survivor of the original band of six, had circled around the warehouse and was kneeling at the building's north-west corner, his back to Stone, trying to locate his adversary.

Stone wanted to take this man alive. He needed information about the strength of Bonner's remaining gang before the inevitable final showdown. He stood and started walking quietly toward the gunman. As Stone approached, the gunman leaned out, fired a shot toward Shadrach's location, then drew back quickly. Stone hoped that the man's preoccupation with Shadrach would allow him to get close enough to demand a surrender before the gunman became aware of his presence. But Stone was no more than half-way to his quarry, still too far for accurate handgun shooting, when instinct told the gunman to turn.

When he did, Stone shouted, 'Drop the gun!' But the gunman ignored the order and as he turned and fired, simultaneously, in a lightning movement, he drew another handgun from the holster on his left hip. With both weapons, he started firing a fusillade toward Stone. A bullet plucked at Stone's left shirt sleeve and he dove for the ground, returning fire. The gunman's weapons were double action, and he fired rapidly, backing up as he fired. His steps took him a foot beyond the protective cover of the warehouse into the alleyway. A shot near Stone's face stung his right cheek with a stone or a bullet fragment, and Stone rolled to his left, firing again. Suddenly there was the roar of Shadrach's shotgun, and the gunman lurched to his left, dropping the pistol in his right hand as the pellets shredded his arm. Stone fired again. At the same time there was another roar, and the gunman went down hard.

Stone got to his feet and walked to the gunman, who lay grimacing in pain and bleeding from a dozen wounds. It was Jones.

Shadrach walked up, reloading the shotgun. As they stood there, over the dying man, Jones looked up and said in a rasping voice, 'It took two of you to get me, didn't it?'

'Yes, it did,' Stone admitted. 'You were good.'

'Damn it, Stone, why didn't you take up Bonner on that offer?' Jones asked.

'I couldn't change the way I am, Jones, no more than you could have changed,' Stone told him. 'How many people does Bonner have? How is he coming after us?'

'You don't expect me to help you, do you?' Jones croaked. He smiled a thin, bloody smile, then his eyes widened and he gasped frantically for air. His last breath came out slowly, like a sigh, only with a gurgle.

'Damn, I needed some information out of him,' Stone spat.

'Sorry, Brim. When he started shooting at you, I had the chance to get up close. When he stepped back from behind the building, I knew I could end it right there.'

'You did the right thing, Shadrach. Couldn't be helped. I doubt we could have taken him alive anyway.' He glanced toward the tool shed. 'Let's check on the ladies.'

They walked back to the tool shed in the corner of the warehouse. Stopping ten feet short of the door, Stone called out, 'It's all over. It's us, Stone and Shadrach.'

The front door opened slowly and Ophelia, her long-barreled pistol in her hand, peered out.

'By God, Stone, I'm glad *that*'s over. I gotta pee!' She headed for the outhouse.

Barbara stepped out, squinting in the rising sun.

'How many did they send?' she wanted to know.

'Half a dozen,' Stone replied.

Barbara looked concerned. 'Are they all dead?'

'Yep, 'fraid so.'

'Good heavens, Stone, the undertaker is going to have to call in some help! Speaking of that,' she said, inspecting his cheek, 'you're hurt.'

'It's nothing, just a nick,' Stone replied. 'But I am thirsty. Got any water around here?'

'There's a big bottle in the office,' Barbara said.

Rejoined by Ophelia, they walked back to the office.

Stone and Shadrach drank eagerly, realizing how dry their mouths had become during the combat they had just been through. As they drank, Barbara glanced out the front window.

'We've got more company,' she warned.

The others moved to the window. A lone rider had turned off the main road and was loping toward the gin.

Twenty yards before reaching the bridge, he reined to a stop and stood up in his stirrups. From where he stopped, he could see two dead horses and three dead men in the road just beyond the bridge, and two saddled, riderless horses grazing in the adjacent field. He looked up at the gin itself, and Stone knew he would be able to see from where he stood the body on the roof of the warehouse.

The rider sat back down in his saddle, gazing at the gin for a long moment, then he turned his horse back toward the main road. Instead of spurring his mount to a gallop, he moved at a gentle lope as if he was in no hurry to deliver his news.

'I can't be sure, but that looked like Deputy Malone,' Stone said.

'He must be the last one walking,' observed Shadrach.

'What now?' Ophelia asked.

'I think it's time to head back into town,' Stone murmured. 'If we give Bonner any more time, he can find some more guns. Or we can sit tight and wait for the Rangers to show up.' He looked at his companions expectantly.

Ophelia harrumphed. 'Well, I for one have got to have a change of clothes and something to eat. Besides, I don't plan to spend the next gun battle sitting in the dark in a musty old tool shed. I'm counting myself in.'

'Come to think of it, I'm kind of hungry myself,' Shadrach agreed.

Barbara dipped her handkerchief in a glass of water and dabbed at the spot of blood on Stone's cheek. 'Well, Stone, looks like we're going to town,' she said.

CHAPTER 14

As the small band approached Ophelia's bagnio, Stone rode ahead to make certain no one was lying in ambush. He rode around the building, but Silver City was virtually deserted.

Inside, they found that Aunt Josie had made coffee and flapjacks.

'How did you know we were coming, Aunt Josie?' Stone wondered, sitting at the kitchen table.

'I din't,' she replied. 'I had to do something to keep my hands from shakin.' I din't know whether any of you was alive or dead. I jus' figured one way or t'other, somebody would need the coffee, even if'n it was the undertaker.'

Ophelia chuckled. 'That's what I love about Aunt Josie. She's practical.'

Stone enjoyed the warmth of the coffee all the way down to the pit of his stomach. In a few minutes, he felt his energy begin to return.

'I'd better get on into town and see if I can find out what Chalmers and Bonner are up to,' he said.

Aunt Josie set a plate of flapjacks and bacon down in front of him, along with a bowl of butter and a pitcher of black strap molasses.

'You cain't go shootin' people on an empty stomach, Mr Brimmer,' she cautioned. 'Better get some of that in you 'fore you heads out.'

Stone looked up and smiled. 'Oh, course you're right, Aunt Josie. An empty stomach makes for an unsteady hand.' He put a glob of butter on the plate and poured the molasses over it, mixing the two with his fork. In a few moments, he had bolted a half-dozen flapjacks. He took a last long gulp from his coffee cup and stood up. He had brought Jones's gun-belt along with him, and he pulled one of the pistols from its holster and hefted it. It was a Colt 1877 double action .41 caliber Thunderer. Stone replaced the expended rounds and stuck the pistol in his belt.

'I agree on one thing with the late Mr Jones,' he said. 'He had excellent judgement in handguns.'

Barbara smiled. 'In other words, he chose the same brand of six-shooter that *you* carry, right?'

'Right,' came Stone's response.

'What are you going to do, Stone?' Ophelia asked, concern in her voice.

'If I can run down some eyes and ears, first I'm going to find out where Chalmers and Bonner are, and second, how many men they have left.'

'Then what?'

'Make some more plans.'

'Don't try it alone, Stone,' Ophelia warned.

Stone turned and looked at the two women. 'All right,' he said. 'Give me forty-five minutes, then come on into town. Stay off California Street! Pull into the alley at the back of the Cowboy's Rest Hotel. I'll meet you there.'

Stone went into the parlor, where Shadrach was keeping watch, and quickly told him his plans.

'We'll be there,' Shadrach said.

Srone walked back through the kitchen to the back door, touching Barbara's cheek as he passed her chair.

'Just a darned minute, Stone,' she said.

136

Barbara got to her feet and threw her arms around Stone's neck, pressing her body into his. Despite her sore lip, she pressed her lips hard to his. Her tongue probed his mouth hungrily. Releasing him and stepping back, she said, 'That's to remind you I've got a big Saturday night planned myself. Don't stick your neck out too far.'

'Hell's kitchen, woman!' he replied. 'That kind of thing could make a man forget his religion, if he had one.'

'Get this thing over with, Brim,' she said, as he turned to go. Tears of exhaustion were starting to well up in her eyes. 'We've got some living to do,' she added softly.

Stone rode into town at a trot, turning off California Street and taking a dirt alley that led to the rear of the hotel. He put his horse in the stable out of sight but left it saddled. When he walked in the back door, the sleepy desk-clerk's eyes grew wide in fright.

'Oh, my land!' the clerk blurted. 'You ain't goin' to hurt me, are you?'

'Why would I want to hurt you?' Stone asked, puzzled.

'The sheriff put out the word that you was a mad dog killer, and everyone was 'sposed to shoot you on sight,' the clerk explained shakily, half crouching behind the reception desk.

'Don't believe everything you hear,' Stone growled. 'Where's Newt?'

The clerk blinked his eyes at the question. 'Newt? Oh, you mean the boy.'

'Yes, that's what I said.'

The clerk bustled from behind the desk and opened a closet door. Newt looked up from his bedroll sleepily, squinting in the light. 'What is it?' he asked. 'I jus' got to sleep.'

'Mr Stone wants to see you,' the clerk said, his eyes darting from side to side.

'Brimstone?' the boy cried delightedly, jumping up. 'Yessir, Mr Brimstone. What can I do for you?'

'What's this Brimstone business?' Stone asked.

'Well, that's what everybody is calling you now. That's what old Bennie Lee Chandler was calling you when Boss Bonner shot him.'

'Bonner shot Bennie Lee? My God! What for?' Stone cried, horrified.

'I was right there,' Newt said proudly. 'When the word got out 'bout you bustin' outta gaol, I went on up to the Lone Star and hung around. There was lots of 'citement, and men with guns runnin' all round. The sheriff was fit to be tied.'

'But what about Bennie Lee?' Stone insisted.

'Well, he was in the Lone Star 'cause he had some money, and he was drinkin' that cheap crack-skull, and ever one was talkin' 'bout you 'scaping and bustin' everybody up. Ol' Bennie Lee thought it were funny and was laughin' and slappin' his knee. Then later on, that Mr Smith what works for Boss Bonner come in, and he'd been to the sawbones and got patched up, and you couldn't hardly tell who it was 'cause of his face bein' so swoll up and the bandages and all. Well, ol' Bennie Lee starts cackling and laughing again and saying that Brimstone has brought hellfire to Rio Diablo and they were all gonna roast on a fiery spit. 'Bout that time, somebody comes in and says that two deputies are dead over at the Carrington house. The sheriff says, 'Oh, God, what am I gonna tell my sister?' Ol' Bennie Lee starts cackling and slapping the bar and saying "I tol' you so", and that's when Mr Bonner got mad sompin' awful. He grabbed Bennie Lee and shoved him outside into the street and drew out his six-shooter and said, 'Shut up, you drunk old bastard.' Bennie Lee says 'Whut you gonna do, shoot me? It don't matter 'cause Brimstone is bringin' hellfire, and he's gonna come finish

138

you off.' Right then, Mr Smith walked out and handed Bennie a pistol. I was right thar, so I seen everthing. Bennie just looked kinda surprised and he was holdin' the pistol upside-down by the butt and Boss Bonner shoots him twice. Then he walks back in and says to the sheriff, "It was self-defense," and the sheriff said, "You're right, you got witnesses." '

Stone was silent for a few moments after Newt had finished his narrative. He fought to get his rage under control. Finally, he found his voice and spoke evenly to Newt.

'Newt, I want you to do something for me.'

Newt was delighted. 'Yessir. What is it?'

'I want you to go on down to the Lone Star and see if anyone is still inside or if you see any activity at all. Look for horses, because if there's some men up in Bonner's office, their mounts will be tied up outside. Remember everyone you see. Understand?'

'You betcha, Mr Brimstone,' Newt answered cheerily, and looked at Stone's hands expectantly.

Stone took a two-bit piece from his pocket and gave it to the boy. 'Half now, half on delivery,' he said.

Beaming, Newt ran to the door and down the street.

Stone had forgotten about the clerk. The man was standing there speechless after hearing Newt's story.

'My Lord,' the clerk said in wonder, 'what kind of people are they that would do a thing like that?'

'The worst there is,' Stone said softly.

Stone went to the front door and peered out. It was still early for the saloon district to be active, and only a few people could be seen moving about. After what the desk-clerk had told him, Stone decided not to venture out before it was necessary. He didn't want to run the risk of meeting a do-gooder, or some cowboy anxious to make a name for himself.

Fifteen minutes later, Newt burst in the front door, grinning. Stone produced another coin and pressed it into the boy's hand.

'Well?' he prompted.

'The Lone Star is the only saloon open this morning. The sheriff and Boss Bonner are sittin' at a table at the back of the room. They's three men with 'em, that Mr Smith and ol' Otis that's big and mean with big bushy eyebrows, and the one deputy the sheriff has got that's still walkin'.'

'Malone?'

'Yep, that's him.'

'Did you go in?'

'Yep, I ast the bartender, who looked awful sleepy, if he had any chores to do 'cause I was needin' breakfast.'

'What were they doing when you went in?'

'They's jus' sittin' there lookin' like they's at a funeral. The sheriff was sippin' whiskey and lookin' like the hangman was comin' for 'im. That Mr Smith was sittin' there with his one good eye almost swoll shut, but I heard him say, "Boss, why don' you go on up to your office and get some rest?" And ol' Boss Bonner say, "hell no, there ain't but one way out of there. I'm goin' to stay here so's I can see who's comin'." 'Bout that time, Boss Bonner looks over and sees me and hollers and says, "What's that brat doin' in here? Get him outta here!" So's the bartender tole me to skeedaddle, and I did.'

Stone smiled. 'As usual, Newt, you are a gold mine of information. When you grow up, you'll make a good lawman.'

Stone was standing near the rear of the lobby, facing the front. As the words were out of his mouth, Stone saw a shadow against the hotel's front window. He grabbed Newt and ducked to the floor just as a shot shattered the window.

'Damn, I got careless,' he thought to himself as he drew and fired toward where he had seen the shadow. 'Get out of here, Newt. Get to the stable and hide.'

Newt bolted for the back door and Stone fired two more shots at the front of the hotel, then turned and ran for the door himself. Immediately to the right of the back door, the rear wall of the building was recessed to provide for a veranda. As he passed through the door, Stone cut to the right and around the corner. He wanted to take his man alive, if it were possible.

Newt made it through the stable door and was closing it behind him when Smith erupted through the back door too quickly for Stone to use his billy. Seeing the door closing, Smith fired at it twice, chest high. Stepping from his cover, Stone yelled, 'Drop it, and stay right where you are!'

Smith froze, his gun hand still extended in front of him.

'I said, drop the gun!' Stone repeated. 'Don't make me shoot you in the back.'

Without moving, Smith said, 'You wouldn't have gotten away with this if I had two good eyes, Stone.'

'I know,' Stone answered. 'You're good. You picked up on the boy. I should have expected that.'

'Where's Jones?' Smith asked, a note of dread in his voice.

'He died early this morning,' Stone answered.

Smith was silent for a moment, then he said, just above a whisper, 'Did he check out in smoke?'

'Yep, firing with both hands.' Stone heard the breath catch in Smith's throat, something like a sob. 'Just drop the gun and unfasten your gun-belt,' he said. 'You'll get a fair trial.'

'Is that what you always tell people you arrest, Stone?' Smith chuckled, then added sarcastically, 'Or should I say, "Brimstone"?'

Smith suddenly bent forward, his gun hand swung downward and to his rear as he fired blindly. Stone dodged to the right, and the shot hit the door facing. Smith was spinning and firing without aiming, trying desperately to keep Stone off balance until he could bring his one good eye into line for a sighted shot. Stone didn't wait, but fired at the turning figure. The shot stopped Smith's spin and he staggered, thumbing off another shot into the ground. Stone fired again and Smith staggered backward against the stable wall, fired once more then toppled forward on his face. Stone walked over and looked at what was left of Smith. His first shot had hit Smith in his left shoulder, smashing the bone. The second shot had entered his chest through the breastbone, and killed him.

Stone went to the stable entry door and opened it, half afraid of what he might see inside. 'Newt?' he called. 'Newt?'

'Yessir, Mr Brimstone,' came the answer from the loft. Some hay trickled off the edge of the loft and Newt's face appeared, upside-down, looking at Stone.

'I was worried,' Stone said.

'Don't you worry, Mr Brimstone,' Newt said cheerily as he scrambled down the ladder. 'I dodged to my left as soon as I closed that door and got flat on the ground. Soon as I heard you talkin', I shinnied up the ladder and waited up here.'

'Good thinking, Newt.' Stone smiled. 'You're thinking more like a lawman every day.'

Still beaming, Newt said, 'Here's your friends, too late to help out with the shootin'.'

Shadrach and Ophelia drove up on the buckboard with Barbara riding just behind.

'We heard the shots,' Barbara said, with relief. 'It looks like it turned out all right.'

142

Shadrach brought the buckboard to a halt and walked over to Smith's body.

'Lordy, his face *is* a mess,' he observed, in wonder. 'How could he even see to shoot?'

'He couldn't, at least not like he needed to. I had the edge,' Stone said. 'You can say one thing for him. He was on the job to the last, even though he shouldn't have been. Too bad he was on the wrong side.'

Shadrach pointed at Newt. 'I see you been using your barefooted telegraph. Find out anything?'

'Yes. Thanks to Newt, we know that Chalmers is down to one deputy. With Smith dead, Bonner is down to one bully, a big fellow, probably one of those at the gaol last night. They're waiting up at the Lone Star. And I found out Bonner killed Bennie Lee Chandler last night.'

Ophelia gasped. 'Oh, my Lord, what in the world for?'

'He was rubbing too much salt in their wounds, and Bonner's composure was starting to fray,' Stone murmured. 'Now, I think it's time for some of that hellfire that Bennie was asking me about.'

'Are we ready?' Ophelia asked.

'As ready as we'll ever be,' Stone told her. 'Shadrach, you go on up to the back of the Lone Star with your scattergun, and watch for anybody going in or out. Barbara, you and Ophelia give us about three minutes, then drive the buckboard up the street and stop across from the Lone Star, but not right in front. I want them to know you are there. Barbara, you have the carbine?'

'Right here,' Barbara affirmed.

'Well, you two wanted to be in on the end of it, so this is your chance. Ophelia, you still have that hog leg you were carrying?'

Ophelia pulled the long-barreled Smith & Wesson out of her oversized handbag. 'I'm ready,' she answered.

Stone reloaded his .45 and returned it to its holster. He

adjusted Jones's pistol in his belt to a more comfortable position, then said quietly, 'Let's move.'

He and Shadrach walked through the hotel to the front door. The hotel clerk was nowhere to be seen. Outside, they turned to the right and started walking east. The street was virtually deserted. Preparation for the day's business had not yet started along 'saloon row'.

At the next corner, Shadrach turned to the right toward the alley that ran at the back of the row of saloons in the next two blocks.

Stone walked up the boardwalk under a gray, lowering sky. The air was unusually warm and close for the time of year, a sure sign that bad weather was on its way. Too, he felt an unaccustomed weariness in his body, and he knew it wasn't entirely physical. He had killed more men in two days than he had in five years as a law officer, and the thought of those wasted lives nagged at him. Now he was going to kill again, or be killed by a man who considered human life as expendable as water.

He was a block away from the Lone Star when he heard a rig coming up the street behind him. Ophelia steered the buckboard past, while Barbara looked at him with a mixture of affection and dread. The rig passed the Lone Star, then pulled to the boardwalk two doors down, and stopped. Ophelia and Barbara stepped down and crouched behind the buckboard. Barbara had her father's carbine at the ready. The stage was set.

Suddenly, Stone could hear light, rapid footsteps behind him on the boardwalk. He turned and saw that Newt was trailing him.

'Newt, get out of here!' he scolded. 'This is not a place for a boy. You can get hurt anywhere around me.'

Newt stopped and grinned. 'I got to see this, Mr Brimstone. I got a feelin' this is goin' to be a day to tell my grandchillun about.'

In no mood to argue with a stubborn street urchin, Stone said, 'At least get across the street and stay out of the line of fire.'

Newt beamed happily and trotted across the street, hopping over the horse droppings and taking up a position on the boardwalk, almost directly across from Stone.

Stone started to step off the boardwalk into a side street, when he saw both Ophelia's and Barbara's heads turn to their right. They were looking up at the second floor of the building that faced the Lone Star, across California Street. It was obvious to Stone that both had heard something. The building facing the Lone Star housed the Maverick Saloon. Stone quickly surveyed the building's façade, and saw that a second-floor window was open by about a foot.

He looked back at the two women. Both were looking at him and pointing to the open window. No one could approach the front of the Lone Star without exposing himself to an easy shot from that window. If he approached the Lone Star from the rear, where Shadrach now stood guard, he would allow Bonner to escape through the front door and put the women in danger from two directions. He had no choice but to put the ambusher out of action before he went after Bonner himself.

Stone stepped into California Street and walked briskly across the street and down a narrow alley between two saloons. At the back of the buildings, he cut to the right and trotted down to the rear of the Maverick Saloon. He approached the back door slowly, listening for any activity inside. He tried the door, and found that it was latched. The lock felt lightweight. He leaned against the door with his full weight. He was rewarded by a random series of cracks and scraping sounds.

'Sheriff Brimstone?'

Stone whirled around, drawing his .45 at the same time. It was Newt!

'What in the hell are you doing here?' Stone growled in a rasping whisper, his heart pounding.

The boy jumped back, startled by the viciousness in Stone's voice.

'I, er, I jest wanted to see if I could hep,' he stammered, close to tears.

Stone struggled for calm, then spoke. 'As long as you are here, yes you can help. I want you to tell Miss Barbara and Ophelia something.'

Newt brightened quickly. 'Yessir. What is it?'

'I want you to go around this way, not the way you came, and tell the ladies this: In five minutes from now, fire two shots. They can be in the air or into the ground, but two shots one right behind the other. Got that?'

Newt beamed. 'We are goin' to give you cover so's you can sneak up on that man in the window, ain't we?'

'Yes, you are,' Stone said. 'And tell the ladies to get inside or under some kind of cover, in case the shooting makes someone nervous.'

'I'm on my way,' Newt said, as he darted away.

Stone watched the boy run up the alley and disappear. A wave of guilt rolled over him as he realized that he was using two women and a boy to help him fight a band of ruthless killers. 'My God, how did I get into this?' he asked himself. But then he remembered the faces of Grady and Bennie Lee, two innocents who died because of the evil that dominated this town, and he knew he had no choice but to take the fight to his enemy.

CHAPTER 15

Stone put his shoulder against the door again. This time, the flimsy latch gave way, and the door swung open into a storage room. He entered quickly, closed the door, and stood motionless. He listened for the sound of footsteps in the almost empty building, the signal that whoever was waiting on the second floor had heard the latch give way and was coming to investigate. Hearing nothing, Stone ventured out of the storage room into the main room of the saloon.

Like the Lone Star across the street, the Maverick had a stairway on one side, leading to a balcony that circled three quarters of the main room. At the rear and at the front of the building were rooms that opened on to the balcony, rooms used for private card games or to allow the saloon's bar girls to 'entertain' customers. To surprise the gunman, Stone knew he would have to climb the stairs, then walk from the saloon's rear to the front along the balcony, which offered no cover except for the thin, decorative spindles supporting the railing. If the gunman suddenly threw open the door and started shooting, the entire matter might end there, one way or the other.

Stone climbed the stairs slowly, placing his feet on the outer edge of each step to minimize squeaks from the old wood. He remembered that two windows opened on to

147

the street from the second floor. The open window would be in the room on the right-hand side as he faced it. He mounted the stairs with his body turned sideways, to keep an eye on that door.

When Stone reached the balcony, he paused momentarily to listen. There were no noises from the street or from the rooms in front. He tiptoed around the balcony, to the front of the building. Taking care to be as quiet as possible, he reached the right-hand door and flattened himself against the wall beside it. He had only moments to wait. The two shots cracked the peacefulness of the morning in California Street, and Stone leaned back and kicked the door open.

Deputy Malone was on one knee, his back to the door, his head half-way out the window. When the door crashed open, the six-shooter dropped from the deputy's right hand and both his hands went into the air. Without turning around, he said, 'Don't kill me, Stone, Don't kill me.'

'Stand up and turn around,' Stone ordered.

Malone did as he was told. When he faced Stone, he half-smiled and said, 'No sooner than I had stuck my head out that window to see what was going on, I realized I'd been aced and you were at my back. What happened to Smith?'

'You can visit him at Grimsby's later on,'

'What about Jones?'

'He's out of it, too. He and those others that Bonner sent out to the cotton gin,' Stone informed him. 'They're all dead.'

Malone shook his head in resignation. 'I was afraid of that. When I rode out to the cotton gin, there were dead men as far as I could see. I came back and told the sheriff and Bonner to give it up and get out of town, but they wouldn't listen. They knew you'd be coming for them, and they wanted me to pick you off when you showed.'

'What's your choice, Malone?'

'Stone, I haven't cared for what's been going on this town for a long time, but it paid well and I never had the gumption to walk away. Now it's not just a question of money; it's a question of living or dying.'

Malone's right hand moved slowly down to his chest. He removed his deputy's badge and tossed it on the floor.

'There's no way anyone can promise me enough money that I'm willing to die to save Bonner's ass. I'm out of it. Let me live, and I'll leave Texas. Your argument's with Bonner and Chalmers, anyway.'

'Get rid of the rest of your weapons,' Stone said.

Relief swept over Malone's face. With two fingers he pulled a pocket pistol from his jacket and let it drop to the floor. Then he pulled a knife with a six-inch blade from his boot. It joined the guns on the floor.

'That's it,' he said.

Stone motioned him toward the door with his pistol, and walked behind him. They walked down the stairs and to the saloon's front door.

'Put your hands down, open the door and go out. Walk to the left, past the ladies at the buckboard. I plan either to kill Bonner, or to arrest him and hold him for Illinois authorities. I'll either kill or arrest Chalmers, and let him stand trial here in Rio Diablo. Get out of town and you are on your own. On the other hand, if they kill me, then you can do whatever you're inclined. Understood?'

'Understood,' Malone said.

Malone opened the door cautiously and stepped through it, closing it gently. Then he turned and walked east along the boardwalk. Ophelia and Barbara watched in surprise as an unarmed Malone walked past them, tipping his hat.

Chalmers suddenly erupted through the Lone Star's swinging doors.

'Malone,' he yelled across the street at his former deputy's back. 'Where in hell are you going?'

Malone continued his unhurried walk, without looking back at his former boss.

'Damnit!' Chalmers screeched. 'You get back here, or I'll have you locked up!'

Malone stopped and turned.

'By who, C.J.?' he yelled back. 'You're plumb out of deputies.' He laughed, then turned and continued on his way.

Chalmers's face flushed red as he sputtered at Malone's jibe. He looked across the street at the two ladies and Newt standing behind the buckboard, and he said with a tone of panic, 'Where's Stone?' Then he disappeared back inside.

Stone walked out the back door of the Maverick and retraced his steps up the alley to California Street. He cautiously peered out at the street, then strolled across it. He marched deliberately to the Lone Star, and stopped short of the window.

He heard Bonner shouting inside. 'Chalmers! Where in hell do you think you are going? Get your ass back here!'

Stone hurriedly stepped past the window and sidled up to the door.

There was silence for a few moments, then he heard Chalmers cry out, 'There's another one at the back with a scattergun. Oh, Jesus!'

Despite himself, Stone could not suppress a smile at the almost comic stage-play desperation in Chalmers's voice. He cautiously peered around the edge of the door and saw Bonner at the rear of the saloon, berating Chalmers. Then Bonner turned, saw Stone, raised a double-barreled shotgun and cocked the hammers. Stone pulled back as a shotgun blast hit the swinging doors, blowing them open and throwing wood splinters into the air. A second blast shattered the window behind him.

'That's his two,' Stone thought, and jumped back into the doorway, pistols at the ready.

Bonner tossed the shotgun aside and grabbed a handgun from a nearby table. Stone started to fire, but Otis, the big man, fired from the back of the room and the slug sizzled past Stone's ear, sending him dodging out of the doorway. Stone reached around the edge of the door with his left hand and fired two shots in the blind to force their heads down, then he stepped through the door. He saw Bonner run to the bar and, with astonishing agility, leap atop the bar, slide across it and drop to the floor behind. Stone fired a shot at the big man, who was crouched behind a heavy table. Then, both Chalmers and Bonner popped up from behind the bar and fired at Stone, but he had again vacated the doorway.

Stone flattened himself against the outside wall and called to the men inside.

'Bonner, Chalmers, give it up! You can't get out of there alive. You'll get a fair trial.'

Bonner yelled, 'Go to hell, Stone!' Then he fired two shots.

Stone was getting impatient. He shouted back, 'Then you're going to die, Bonner. Both of you. There's no reason for either of you to go on living.'

Bonner barked at the big man at the back of the room. 'Otis, what in hell am I paying you for? Kill that son of a bitch, and kill 'im now.'

'I'll kill 'im, Boss,' came the reply.

Stone heard heavy footsteps rumble across the floor, and he realized that Otis was charging across the saloon. Stone slid down the wall to a crouching position, and waited.

The big man came bursting through the swinging doors with a roar, knocking both off their hinges and catapulting one of them into the street. As he charged on to the boardwalk, he fired to his left, hoping to throw Stone off balance but the shot went wild and his momentum carried him into the street.

'Drop the gun!' Stone ordered.

In reply, Otis cocked the hammer on his single-action .44, but Stone fired first, hitting the big man in the leg. Otis grunted in pain and sank to one knee.

'Drop it, Otis!' Stone repeated.

Otis raised the big pistol again. This time, Stone fired into the man's thick body. Otis lurched backward, but recovered and, with a snarl, raised his weapon once more. Realizing that he wouldn't be able to take the man prisoner, Stone fired a kill shot. The slug struck Otis between the eyes and exited through the back of his head. It tore out a fist-sized hole in the skull, and scattered blood, bits of white skull and gray brain tissue in the street. The big man fell backward into the dirt.

Again, Stone called through the door. 'You're out of help, Bonner. Otis is dead.'

Stone heard Chalmers bleat, 'Oh, God. Oh, God!'

'It's time to talk, Bonner. That is, if you want to go on living,' Stone shouted. 'We can make some kind of deal.'

Bonner answered, 'I'll go along with that, but I want to leave Rio Diablo and take my goods with me. It'll be worth a lot to you, Stone.'

'Can't do that, Bonner. Bennie Lee's dead. You've got to stand trial for that.'

Bonner scoffed. 'He was a worthless piece of trash, a drunk. He's not worth the two of us taking the time to talk about him. Let's talk real business, Stone.'

'How about the Duke girl, Bonner, or should I call you *Morley*? Was she a worthless piece of trash too?'

There was a pause as Bonner gathered his wits. 'You're way too smart for your own good, Stone. For your information, she was all sweetness and light and romance until it came time to do what was necessary and she started bridling.'

Stone replied, 'So she had a conscience, eh, Morley? Can't let a thing like that stand in your way, can you? Speaking of that, there's some folks up in Chicago that want to have a chat with you, Morley. I think you better stick around until they get here.'

'OK, OK, you're smart, Stone. And I'm betting that you're smart enough to know a good deal when you hear it.'

'What's that, Bonner?'

'If you can use ten thousand dollars, we can do business, Stone. How about it?'

Stone's lips curled into a sardonic grin. 'What's your proposition, Bonner?'

'I gather my goods from my office. I walk out the back way and disappear, and I hand you ten thousand on the way out.'

'Sounds simple enough,' Stone remarked. 'What's the catch?'

'No catch, Stone. I live, you live, and I'm out of your life and this town for good.'

'What about Chalmers?'

'You can have him, Stone.' Bonner chuckled. 'Somebody has to take the fall. Why not our faithful sheriff?'

Chalmers screamed, 'What are you saying? Take the fall for what? You mean you're gonna run out on me?'

Stone laughed. 'Chalmers, you see what happens? You lie down with dogs, you get up with fleas.'

'I ain't goin' to take this, Bonner,' Chalmers cried. 'Stone! I want to talk to you. I'll tell you whatever you need to know.'

'Looks like our deal is off, Bonner,' Stone shouted. 'You're heading for Illinois.'

Enraged, Bonner bellowed, 'I'll see you in hell first, Stone!'

Stone heard Chalmers talking in plaintive tones, but couldn't make out what he was saying. He heard Bonner's angry voice say something in reply. It sounded to Stone as if Chalmers was ready to break into tears.

Attracted by the gunfire, people had started to gather on the boardwalk in the two blocks to either side of the Lone Star. Stone heard someone ask indignantly, 'Where's the sheriff? Why doesn't he come and arrest this outlaw?' Then he heard another person in the crowd guffaw and say, 'Hell, the sheriff's in the saloon prayin' for his life!' The crowd laughed.

Stone knew he couldn't fire through the heavy wood of the bar with any effect and that the siege could go on for hours. He was aware that if Bonner had messaged friends or professional guns for help the day before, they might be arriving on the train from Fort Worth at any moment so there was a sense of urgency in ending the stand-off. The last time he had fired from the doorway, he had seen a coal oil lantern burning incongruously on the shelf behind the bar. It probably had been lit during Bonner's all-night vigil, and had gone unnoticed in the excitement after the sun rose. Stone saw a way to end the stand-off, risky but effective.

'One last chance, Bonner,' Stone called. 'How about you, Chalmers? If you put your weapons down and come out now, you live. Too many men have died already for me to kill two more. How about it?'

'Go to hell, Stone!' Bonner shouted and fired a shot through the door.

'Remember what I said at the gaol last night, Bonner? I wasn't blowing smoke up your ass. Now one of us is going to die, Bonner, and it's not going to be me.'

Stone reached around the edge of the doorway with

Jones's pistol in his left hand and fired three blind shots, then stepped quickly into the doorway and took careful aim at the lantern. His shot shattered the base of the lamp and struck several whiskey bottles behind the lantern. The burning wick toppled over and ignited the coal oil. The flames quickly licked to the spilled alcohol and spread rapidly.

Stone shouted, 'Here's some hellfire, courtesy of Bennie Lee!'

Stone felt a cool breeze on the back of his neck. Turning, he could see dust and debris being whipped into the air by wind from an approaching thunderstorm. 'Good timing,' he said to himself. 'That should speed things along.'

The fire was gaining strength very fast, climbing up the wall. The old wood construction was ideal for a hungry fire, and the ceiling quickly became involved. Stone heard Bonner shouting at Chalmers again, saying, 'Help me . . . money . . . got to get it out.' Then loud cursing.

Suddenly Chalmers burst out of the saloon door, his hands in the air.

'Don't shoot!' he pleaded. 'I give up. I'll cooperate. Don't kill me.'

Surprised, Stone hesitated. Then he said, 'Chalmers, get down . . . .' but he was interrupted by a shot from inside the saloon. Chalmers grunted and pitched forward off the boardwalk, falling face down in the street, almost on top of Otis's body. He lay very still, and Stone assumed he was dead.

The fire was starting to roar. Stone peered around the edge of the door to see Morley racing up the stairs to his office.

'Don't go up there!' Stone shouted. 'The place is going up, you won't get out.'

As if to answer him, a great gust of wind swept down the

155

street and through the open door and shattered window of the saloon, pushing the blaze up the staircase, to eat the old, oiled wood rapidly. The heat became intense, and Stone stepped away from the building. Several men detached themselves from the crowd and pulled the two bodies in the street away from the fire.

The volunteer fire department came running, pushing and pulling a fire pump, but the intensity and size of the fire had already outstripped the meager stream produced. Someone shouted, 'These buildings are doomed. Let's save the ones in the next block.'

It occurred to Stone that Bonner might have another way out of the building. He ran to the corner and down the side street to the alley, where he joined Shadrach.

'Have you seen Bonner?' he called.

'Yes, he's up there,' Shadrach told him, pointing at the second-floor window.

Stone looked up at the window. He could see Bonner standing there, his hands on the bars, panic distorting his face.

Shadrach said, 'I could see him up there trying to do something. But the flames came up behind him and he can't get out.'

As Stone and Shadrach watched, Bonner tried desperately to loosen the bars that criss-crossed the window. He looked out at the two men and yelled, 'Help me! Help me! Get these bars off! I'll give you twenty thousand, Stone, thirty thousand!'

As he pleaded for help, the flames engulfed the room behind him and his pleas became screams. The flames reached him, and his clothes caught fire. When his hair was alight, his screams no longer sounded human, but instead like the shrieks of a wounded animal. He didn't let go of the bars, and the flames froze his limbs there, his mouth open in a continuing scream. As the flesh of his face blackened, Stone and Shadrach turned away. They ran back to the alley and around to Chisholm Street, to escape the heat and the smoke.

At that moment, the heavens seemed to open and the rain fell in blinding sheets as if to wash away the horrors the men had witnessed. They welcomed the cooling water as they walked back to where the women waited.

The efforts of the volunteer firefighters, aided by the short-lived but intense cloudburst, saved the buildings in the next block. It was noon by the time the firemen were sure the flames would not spread farther. As Stone and his small band watched the remains of a city block smolder, they began to relax for the first time in two days.

They sat on the edge of the boardwalk, relishing the feeling of safety. The Baptist minister walked by, looking at the wreckage, and recognized Barbara. He touched the brim of his hat to Barbara, then addressed Stone.

'Well, young man,' he said, 'you are aptly named. The undertaker has had to hire extra hands to help him haul in the bodies you've left all over the county. The sheriff is dead and an entire city block has been burned to the ground. I was moved to call down God's wrath on you, but I heard him speak to me. I am prevented from calling down vengeance on you because those buildings were all saloons, and the dead men weren't worth the powder and lead it took for you to blow them to hell. The sun shines brighter in this stricken town than it did yesterday, and I suppose we have you to thank for it.' He paused for breath and looked skyward, then intoned, 'The Lord moves in mysterious ways his wonders to perform,' and walked away without another word.

Ophelia said, 'That was an exit line if ever I heard one. I'm going to go get some sleep.' Ophelia and Shadrach bid Stone and Barbara a weary goodbye, and headed back toward Silver City on the buckboard, giving Newt a lift back to the Cowboys' Rest.

'I could use a bath,' Barbara said. 'My hair smells of burned saloon.'

Stone and Barbara walked down the street through lingering smoke to Mom's, and ordered coffee. When Mom brought their coffee and said, 'I swear, mister, when you get even, you get even! I'm just glad that you didn't get so mad you burned down *my* place as well.'

Stone smiled wearily. 'I'd never do that, Mom. I like your cooking too much.'

Mom surveyed Barbara and raised her eyebrows. 'I see that you don't do *anything* half-way, do you son?'

Stone smiled and said, 'My old pappy told me that if a thing was worth doing, it was worth doing well.'

Mom chuckled and said, 'The coffee is on the house.' She glanced out the window. 'Here comes the county judge. Reckon he's going to arrest you or hang a medal on you.'

The judge, a tall, slender man with little glasses on his nose, walked in and put out his hand.

'Stone,' he said, 'I'm Millard Eggleston, county judge. Do you have a moment?'

'I reckon so, Judge, as long as it doesn't interrupt my coffee-drinking,' Stone answered.

'Morning, ma'am,' the judge said to Barbara, touching his hat brim.

Mom brought the judge a cup of coffee. He nodded his thanks and turned to Stone.

'I just saw Judge Hodges leaving town in a big hurry,' he said. 'In case you weren't aware, he was the one who signed the warrant that Chalmers, excuse me, the *late* Sheriff Chalmers, served on you.'

'I didn't know,' Stone said. 'I never got a chance to take a look.'

Judge Eggleston smiled. 'The way I see it, he figured he

was next on your list, Mr Stone, and that thought gave wings to his feet. At any rate, it's good riddance. Anyway, the reason I'm here is because I'm the Cudahey County judge and I head up the County Commissioners' Court. I did some checking on you by telegraph yesterday down to Harris County and found out a lot. I figure that we are going to need a sheriff and I wondered if you were interested in the job.'

Stone frowned, peering into his coffee. 'Judge,' he answered, 'I am flattered by your offer, but right now I don't want to think about that.'

'What do you want to think about?' Barbara asked, putting her hand on his forearm.

'I'm still turning that bath over in my mind,' he answered.

'Why don't we go heat up some water and see what happens?' she suggested.

'Well,' the judge said, standing up, 'you don't have to give me an answer right now. Think about it. We'll talk after you've had some, ah, rest.'

'Sounds good to me,' Stone said. 'I'll look you up, Judge.'

As they hurried out the door, Mom laughed wickedly and shouted, 'You kids be good now. You hear?'